NEVER, NEVER

CALLIE TAYLOR

THE WHUMPY PRINTING PRESS

Dedicated to Elli, whose endless enthusiasm and encouragement for this story helped me to see it through.

CONTENTS

CONTENT WARNINGS

This story contains the following content:
- Heavy gore, including amputation and torture

- Restraints

- Captivity

- Nonconsensual drug use

- Begging for death

If this book isn't for you, no worries! But if it is, we hope you enjoy this story about a very unfortunate captain …

1

LEFT

"Pick a hand."

James eyed his captor, sullen and silent. For two days, he'd been a prisoner in the brig of his own ship. No food, no water, kept bound in the same bent position by rough rope. No idea if the men still loyal to him were even *alive*.

His body ached, his head was pounding, his mouth felt swollen, and here was Peter, first mate turned mutineer, giving him stupid orders.

"*Pick a hand*," Peter said again, sounding annoyed.

"Why?" James spat out, his voice rasping. "Why should I do anything you ask of me?"

Peter clicked his tongue. "Well, now, you don't sound like someone who wants a drink of water."

James scowled. So this was how it was going to be. He'd have to play Peter's games, cave in to his demands, just for the pleasure of keeping himself alive. *Fine.* His life was worth more to him than his pride.

"Left," he said, and Peter's face broke into a smile.

"There we go!" he said, producing a small flask from his hip and unscrewing the lid. He pressed it to James's mouth, and he drank, unable to grasp it himself with his hands tied behind his back. It was taken away too soon.

"Now, you said your left hand?" Peter asked, moving behind him. James tensed as his former first mate cut the hand in question loose in such a way that the other was still tied firmly in place. Traitor or not, Peter was skilled in rope tricks. He gripped his wrist tightly, and James winced as his arm was straightened for the first time in days.

Even with one hand freed, the rest of his body was practically immobilized. Trying to fight at this point would undoubtedly fail. His best hope was to entertain Peter's whims until the traitor let his guard down.

"*Left hand*, *left hand*. Good choice," Peter said, tracing a finger along James's palm, something wild in his eyes. "Now, will you let me cut it off?"

James clenched his jaw. Even though he'd suspected this was the way things were headed, the words were a shock. "*What*?"

"I want to cut off your hand," Peter said. "But only if you tell me to. Will you?"

What kind of game was he playing now? "No. Why would I?"

"Okay!" Peter said brightly, suddenly releasing his arm. James watched him stride out of the room, flexing his fingers. Was that it? Was Peter just trying to mess with his head? He took a shaky breath when the other man returned a few moments later, carrying what looked like a small anvil.

Of course not. Peter's games are never so simple.

The anvil was placed a few feet to James's left, and he felt a shudder run through him when he saw the metal cuff welded to the top. Where had Peter come by such a thing? Had it been the last time the crew made port? He wouldn't know. As a young captain, it seemed a poor choice to mingle with his crew on a friendly level. Better to command respect and leave the befriending to the first mate, he'd told himself after taking the helm of *The Scarlet Merry*. Only now could he see what a mistake that had been.

James was too weak to pull away when Peter seized his hand and could do nothing as he was dragged from the wall, body stretched as far as his restraints allowed, left wrist locked into place atop the anvil.

"I'm going to ask again," Peter said, and his voice wasn't harsh or threatening, just matter-of-fact. "Can I cut off your hand?"

James's heart pounded in his ears, worsening the headache that had nestled between his temples the first day and refused to leave. Should he just say yes? Get whatever Peter had in store over with? Or would he really be spared if he denied the request? He squeezed his eyes shut, thinking of climbing the rigging, steering the ship, engaging in battle. All things better served with two hands intact.

4

"No," he said at last.

"Alright then," Peter said cheerfully, drawing a small knife. Its edge was polished, razor-sharp, and its hilt was shaped in the likeness of a crocodile, scales rippling gold in the dim light of the brig, twin rows of teeth pulled apart to let the blade spill out, as if the beast were breathing fire. James felt his blood run cold as Peter brought it down to trace the outline of his hand, the dead metal eye of the creature watching him without pity.

"That means I get to convince you."

***

Peter started with the ring finger. One long, deep cut along the inside of it, a few more around the circumference, and he was able to set to work on removing the skin.

No amount of begging or threatening would stop him; James found that out within a few minutes. He'd tried to clench his hand into a fist, but Peter struck him against the knuckles with the hilt of the knife and threatened to take an eye if he made this difficult, so he'd given up on protecting the hand and took to screaming instead.

"*Cut it off, cut it off*!" he howled as the finger was reduced to bone and muscle, and then not even that as Peter began to slice away at the tendons.

Peter responded in a calm, friendly voice as he dug the point of the knife into the first joint and began to pry it away, "It's too late for that. You can only tell me to cut it off when I ask you if you're *ready* for it to be cut off."

And so James could only wail helplessly, straining against the bindings that held him in place until his skin burned and bled wherever the rope touched it. He would have been sick if his stomach had anything to give up.

Peter hummed as he carried on, removing more and more of the finger until it was down to the knuckle. He paused then, looking at the bloody space thoughtfully, and for a moment, James dared to hope he was done.

But then Peter jammed the point of the knife into the wound, and James's vision went white with pain. For a blissful few seconds, he knew nothing, *felt* nothing. But when the world came back to him, Peter was holding his thumb.

***

He didn't know how long it took as the process was repeated, the slow filleting of each finger, the piece-by-piece removal of bone. James's mind felt like it had melted into the pain, each new excruciating stroke indistinguishable from the last as he faded in and out of consciousness, barely able to do more than whimper as his body shook and his hand was *taken* from him one slice at a time.

Eventually, he opened his eyes to see everything gone, the remains of his hand sitting amid discarded flesh and gore, blood weeping from hollow knuckles with every thump of his heart. Peter was carving the skin off his palm, still humming a carefree tune, paying no mind to the scarlet that coated his hands, his knife, his clothes. The mouth of the reptilian hilt was red through and through, like the little metal beast had just messily devoured something. In some twisted way, it had.

James let out a sound that was something between a sob and an animalistic whine, and Peter's gaze flicked down.

"Ah, you're awake!" He lifted the knife, twirling it between two fingers. "Now, I hope you remember the rules, because it's your turn again."

His turn. As if they were playing cards. James couldn't speak, couldn't even nod. It had to be over. He couldn't take any more of this slow slicing. *It had to be over.*

"I think you know what I'm going to ask you," Peter continued in a singsong voice. James only stared up at him. His vision was swimming. He had to stay conscious long enough. He had to be able to say the word, just one word.

"*Can I cut off your hand?*"

2

CLARITY

Asleep and awake interchanged so quickly James no longer knew which was which. Both were dark and foggy and full of pain. He began to dread even those short bursts of true unconsciousness; they only meant he'd have to come back to awareness and get used to the agony all over again. His limbs ached endlessly, his body shook, his arm was on fire. All he wanted was for it to stop, to crawl out of his skin and never come back, but nothing would even so much as take his mind off it. His whole world was pain, the pull of the ropes, the memory of Peter's sadistic little smile. The only freedom he could imagine was death, and even that was beginning to sound sweet.

In his moments of clarity, James found himself wishing Peter had seen fit to kill him in the battle that lost him the ship. Wouldn't that have been easier? Wouldn't that have been kinder? Better to die unbound, on his feet, a sword in his hand. Better to die as captain.

James had no conception of how long it had been since the little golden knife had first left its sheath. And how long had it been since he'd been able to glimpse the horizon, the blue of the sea? Time didn't matter anymore, had no consequence. There was no time, there was only the fever of sleep and the haze of wakefulness. He cried for water, for morphine, for someone to shoot him and be *done* with it. The latter two requests were ignored, and so he continued the cycle, now and then rising into moments of awareness, only to be swiftly pulled back under the waves.

After one such spell of peaceful nothingness, James woke to find himself in a bed. Well, sort of a bed. A mat had been placed between him and the wooden floor, a blanket draped over him to form a barricade between his body and the cool sea air. Whoever had done it even had the decency to untie him. Between his next bouts of unconsciousness, he was aware of bandages being changed, the abrasions from the rope being cleaned, water being poured down his throat in a trickle.

Somewhere deep beneath the fog of delirium and pain, this scared him.

Peter was trying to keep him alive. *Why* was Peter trying to keep him alive? The thought added dread to his waking moments and turned his fever dreams to terror. In them, Peter would cut into him again. His leg, his throat, or most often, his hand. Only this time, it kept growing back.

***

Gradually, the fire that enveloped his arm began to cool, his thoughts becoming more lucid. The next time he was visited by whoever had taken to caring for him, he was awake.

Esme Jedediah, Jeddy to the crew of *The Scarlet Merry*, swung the door open, a bowl in her hand and a roll of bandages tucked under her arm. Soft sunlight falling down the stairs from the deck above cast her in an almost ethereal light, setting a glow to her dark skin and turning her tight curls into a halo. The picture of an angel of mercy.

Or destruction. Keeping him alive at a demon's bidding.

She seemed surprised to see James staring at her.

"Looks like your fever's broke," she said in a low voice, dropping to one knee and setting the bowl on the ground next to him.

"How long – " he tried to say, but his voice wouldn't work, his throat creaking with the effort. He tried again. "How long has it been?"

She shrugged, staring down at the bowl. "Somethin' like a week. The captain did a number on you."

His heart sank at her words. *The captain*. He liked Jeddy. Quiet but competent, serious about her job as master gunner. She'd lived practically her whole life at sea. He hadn't seen her during the initial scuffle and had hoped she'd escaped, hoped she hadn't been one of those ready to betray him. But here she was. Calling Peter 'captain.'

She turned her attention to the stump of his left arm, unwinding the stained bandage. He winced as it pulled at the skin, doing his best to choke down a whimper.

"Glad you're finally awake, though," she said as she bunched up the soiled dressing. "I was gettin' tired of listening to your weepin' and moanin'."

James dared to cast a glance at his now-unbandaged arm, his stomach twisting. Crude stitches holding together reddened flesh, blood oozing between them.

Jeddy saw him staring. "Peter left you with a hack-job," she said, dipping a cloth into the bowl beside him. "I had to clean it up after he was done. Slice off the tatters so I could patch it up nicer – "

James was rolled over on his side, dry-heaving, before she could finish. *Slice off the tatters*, just a few more cuts, a few more pieces *removed* ...

She eased him back onto the mat. The effort had left his head swimming, tears streaming down his face as concern lined Jeddy's.

"Easy now, just breathe and you'll be alright, cap – " She caught herself, glancing back down at the bowl. "Mm. You should probably have somethin' to eat," she mumbled, wiping the wound with the doused cloth. Whatever was in the bowl, it stung, and James found himself suppressing another whine.

His stomach twisted again at the mention of food. He was hungry, outright *starving*, but he didn't know if he could keep anything down. Unbidden came the memories of dinners with the crew, celebrations after a successful raid or a good trade, tables full of fish and bread and wine, sometimes fruit, sometimes sweets, always laughter and loud, jovial voices. He'd always taken so much care to be a part of it while maintaining a bit of distance. If they saw him as a friend, a peer, how would he ever maintain order? Respect?

Now it seemed those things hardly mattered. Peter had always sat among the others, laughing with them, sharing stories. He'd been with the *Merry* a scant two years, and yet it seemed the crew would follow him anywhere. Why hadn't James *seen* that they would follow him anywhere?

Jeddy finished cleaning his arm, rebandaged it with deft fingers, and produced a waterskin. "Drink," she said, and he did. The fingers of his right hand were too weak to keep a good hold on it, but Jeddy seemed to anticipate this and helped him keep it steady, tilting his head up with her free hand.

He felt like an infant, frail and helpless. He hated it, but his body betrayed him. It needed the water, the helping hand. His base instincts insisted he try to survive. Jeddy re-stopped the waterskin once it was apparent he could drink no more, pulling aside her worn leather jacket to hook it back onto her belt.

"Keep awake a while longer. I'll bring you some soup," she said, pushing herself up from the floor. James nodded, trying to sit up, but finding himself too weak to even lift his head. Jeddy saw this and knelt back down, helping him into a seated position and moving him so his back was supported by the wall.

The motion made his vision swim. He felt *hollow*, carved out of something far more delicate than flesh and bone. Jeddy laid his mutilated arm on his lap, and the limb throbbed with the shift in position.

"Now, as I said, keep awake." She stood again, making to leave.

"Wait. Jeddy." As much as he dreaded the answer he was about to seek, James couldn't let himself stew in the unknown any longer. He took a breath to steel himself. "Why is he letting you help me? Why … why am I not *dead*?" He didn't know what he wanted to hear; there didn't seem to be a good outcome. Expertise or an execution in front of the crew, neither would be pleasant in Peter's hands.

Jeddy fixed him with a grim look. "I thought you'd figure it out on your own," she began, turning the door handle. It opened with a soft creak.

"Peter ain't done with you yet."

3

— · —

PLAYING GAMES

A week went by, at least as far as James could tell. A week of gentle wooden creaks as the ship bobbed on the waters, of straining to hear the voices above deck, of dark air that only ever brightened when the door to the brig swung open. James filled most of his time with sleep and, on the rare occasion the pain in his arm dulled enough for him to think, tried to distract himself with memories. Only the good ones, when he could help it. He tried to recall days of his youth, sailing aboard a merchant ship, long before he'd turned pirate. Sun, storms, and hard work; learning the ins and outs of a ship and earning his place aboard it. He'd been nineteen when he abandoned *King's Joy* for *The Scarlet Merry*, back when Greyson was still captain and James was only a deckhand. Years turned him to second mate, then first, then at last to captain when Greyson decided it was time to retire. And now he'd gone from captain to prisoner, faster than a person could sink to the bottom of the sea.

His memories were tinged with bitterness by the fate he now found himself in, but they brought him less pain than his body did, at least temporarily, and were better than fearing the future.

In his time of rest, Jeddy was his sole visitor, bringing water and a thin soup, checking his wound and changing the bandages daily. When the pain had ebbed enough, James was able to take a more thorough stock of his situation.

His ankles were still cuffed together, a small link of chain between them, connected to a longer one that spanned several feet and was bolted to the wall. As if he could *stand* on his own, much less try to run. The fever and lack of food had incapacitated him as well as any binding could. If the ship were docked and every restraint removed, James doubted he could even make it to the door.

Jeddy didn't speak much during her visits, only ever commenting on his condition. He didn't dare ask what Peter had in store for him, and even if he did, he wasn't sure she'd be able to answer. Peter was unpredictable. It was impossible to pin down what he might be thinking at any given moment.

Even the mutiny had come out of nowhere. There had been no preamble, no murmurs of discontent. The traitors aboard *The Scarlet Merry* had simply sprung, outnumbering the loyal few, quickly overpowering their former captain and tossing him below.

If only he'd had just another instant of awareness of the plot. He could've fought back harder. They could've killed him, he could've escaped the pain, the *dread* he was currently stewing in.

The food Jeddy brought did little to help him regain his strength, and he couldn't even look at his arm without wanting to empty his stomach. He could feel the ghost of his left hand, nonexistent wounds still being dealt to the nonexistent appendage.

He was blinking away sleep when the door opened, but this time it wasn't Jeddy standing at the entrance.

It was Peter.

The false captain strode into the room, stopping to loom over James, who glowered up at him. Afraid as he might be of what came next, he couldn't find it in him to cower before his captor. To beg for mercy, for release, for a swift death. Not yet. If a threat presented itself, if Peter started cutting into another part of him, James didn't think he'd be able to stop himself from begging. He knew he wouldn't survive a repeat of his hand, and didn't care to die screaming.

"I'm glad to see you up," Peter said, crouching next to him. James did not reply, but his former first mate didn't seem to mind, taking hold of his arm and rotating it so the stump was facing him. James held his breath as the other man began unwinding the bandage.

"Hm," he said, tracing his finger along the stitching. James flinched back, but Peter's grip only tightened.

"*Shh*, no, no," he said, voice barely above a whisper, a mockery of soothing. "Don't try and pull away. Remember what I said would happen if you made this difficult." He closed one eye. "Remember?"

James nodded, feeling his resolve crumble away.

"Say it. Tell me what will happen."

"You'll ... you'll take an eye," James said, his voice like still water, like the slightest ripples could set Peter off.

"That I will," Peter said, grinning. "I wonder how long I could make that last. What do you think? Will you let me put it out right away? Or will I have to cut out a few pieces first? I've seen the inside of an eye before, but never a live one. I wonder how many layers I can cut off if I'm careful. I wonder how much it will bleed – "

James's chest hitched, a sob escaping and cutting Peter short. He could imagine it. He could *feel* it. The golden crocodile sinking its teeth into the socket, biting and chewing and eating as his vision went red, then disappeared. The heat of tears trailed down his face.

"Shhh, don't cry," Peter said softly, wiping away the tears with a gentle hand. His thumb lingered under James's right eye, pressed in lightly. "Does that mean you'll let me do it?"

His chest felt like it was freezing over. "If ... only if I'm difficult. You said – "

"Yes. If you're difficult. Will you let me cut your eye out? I'll let you pick which one." He pressed his finger deeper when James was silent. "*Say it.*"

James nodded, more tears spilling onto his cheeks. In that moment, they felt like blood. "If I make it difficult. I-I want you to put out my eye."

"There, that wasn't so hard," Peter said, pulling away. He stood, letting James's wounded arm drop onto the wooden floor. The pain shooting up from the stump was *nothing* compared to the fate James felt he'd only barely avoided.

"Now, aren't you curious?" Peter said. "Have you been wondering why I did it? Surely you have." He nudged James with his boot. "Yes? No?"

James swallowed, waiting until he was sure he could steady his voice. "Yes," he said. He *was* curious, but he was already anticipating another torturous 'game.' Peter rarely did anything without some sly plan in the works.

"Guess why," Peter said.

"I don't know," James replied.

"Well, *obviously* you don't, but I want you to guess."

James stared up at him, silent as his mind scrambled for whatever answer Peter would deem correct. Peter smiled down at him. Closed one eye.

"You – you got bored," James said quickly, and Peter tapped his nose.

"Good guess! Good, and *almost* right." Without warning, he brought his foot down hard, stomping on the remains of James's left arm and dragging a scream from his throat.

"Almost isn't good enough," Peter continued. His tone was conversational, like they were talking over tea. "Would you like to guess again?"

"*Hnng* – no." James clutched his arm. The stump where it now ended throbbed horribly. Some of the stitched skin had broken, blood trailing down toward his elbow.

"Alright then, suppose I'll tell you." Peter cleared his throat, spread his arms in a grand gesture. "*The fountain of youth.*"

That was enough to cut through the pain, if only for an instant.

"What?" James said.

"I knew you'd think it mad," Peter said. "And I knew you'd say no. You'd say it was a myth. A fairy tale."

"It *is*," James hissed.

"And I'll chase it forever if that's what it takes," Peter said.

James couldn't help but wonder if this was yet another game, a trick to quicken the loss of his sanity. The fountain of youth. It was a myth, *only* a myth. *The Scarlet Merry* would rot in the water before such a thing could be found.

"I hope you're not disappointed," Peter said. "You didn't think the mutiny was about you, did you?"

"If – if it wasn't, then why – ?"

"Why cut off your hand?" He grinned. "Well, it's like you said. I was bored."

James pressed his back into the wall as the other man leaned down, willing it to break and spill his body into the sea. Peter leaned over him, brushing a strand of dark hair out of his face.

"Now, you'd better get some rest. I believe I'll be bored again quite soon."

4

— · —

A FORM OF SURRENDER

"Why you?"

Jeddy visited him a few hours after Peter had gone, to tend his arm and help him eat another bowl of thin soup. The conversation with his former first mate had left him shaken. Beyond the threat of further mutilation, it had been made clear that he had only been left alive on a whim. To him, that meant he could also be *killed* on a whim and tortured whenever Peter was struck with inspiration. And if he stayed chained down here, such a fate would only be a matter of *when*.

Jeddy raised an eyebrow at his question, wordlessly asking what he meant. James swallowed down another spoonful of his meal.

"You're a gunner, not a nurse," he said. Not just a gunner, but the *Merry*'s master gunner. Quick behind a cannon, quicker to sort any problems that arose during combat and issue the commands to turn the tide of the fight. A soft-spoken woman whose voice hardened and sharpened in the heat of battle, whose eyes came alive when she was protecting her ship. A fighter.

Jeddy shrugged at his question. "The doc jumped ship when the fightin' started. I know my way around a wound, so I volunteered after ... " She pressed her lips together tightly. "After we heard the screamin'."

James nodded, silent. He knew it was stupid, the shame that rolled through him at her words, but the thought of his crew – his *former* crew – listening to him wailing, crying, *begging* for it to end ...

He elected to change the subject.

"Peter said he's after the fountain of youth. He ... he just needed a ship and crew to get there. Are you with him on that?"

She shrugged again. "Dunno. I go where the *Merry* goes."

"No matter who's at the helm," James said. She didn't answer at first, stirring the bowl of soup and staring into the whirlpool of broth she'd created until the liquid stilled.

"You were a good captain," she said at last. "I was sorry this happened, but Peter has too strong a sway over the others, and I won't leave this ship." She didn't look at him, hands tightly wound around the bowl. "But as I said, you were a good captain. I can get you something to help. Morphine. Scale. Rum. Something to put you out of your wits until it's over – "

"No," James cut her off. "For the pain, *yes*, but if you only want me to be lost in myself ... no."

"Peter can be cruel, we both know it," Jeddy said. "I'd surely have nightmares if I knew what else he had in store for you."

He was tempted for a moment. How easy would it be to surrender himself to substance, to die a little less painfully? It might even spite Peter. The other man wouldn't glean so much joy from hurting him if he wasn't even coherent enough to know where he was.

Yet it *would be* surrendering. Giving up on any hope, any chance of catching his captor off-guard and escaping. As small as that spark of hope was, it was still there, and he didn't want to lose a chance to fan it into a flame.

He clenched his jaw, placing his right hand on Jeddy's forearm.

"If you want to help me, bring me more food. Bread. Meat if you can." He was well past the fever, but still kept on the brink of starvation by the scant amounts of soup. No doubt part of Peter's plan to keep him weakened.

Jeddy frowned. "The captain won't like it ... but I can try."

And for the next few days, she did. Chunks of fish hidden within the broth he'd been surviving on, biscuits smuggled in with the bandages. He found it almost touching that she'd risk trouble for him. Hells, she'd asked to care for him in the first place. Before she'd admitted to volunteering, James had assumed she was only tending him on Peter's orders. If she hadn't offered to care for him, would Peter have sent someone crueler? Now that his former first mate's true colors had flown,

James had no doubt there were cruel men to be found onboard. At the last port, Peter had hired on new hands, *strangers*, and like a fool, James had trusted his judgment.

The realization that it could have been so much worse sat sour in his gut, and despite where he was and how hopeless it all seemed, in that moment he was endlessly grateful for Jeddy, mutineer or not. It wasn't about Peter for her. It was about the ship. She'd already been a crew member when James had inherited the *Merry* from her previous captain, and she'd been aboard longer than even he had. So in a way, he could understand. Jeddy wasn't a traitor; her loyalties would always lie with *The Scarlet Merry* herself.

***

On her next visit, Jeddy's expression was grimmer than usual.

James thought of asking her what was wrong, if there was some kind of trouble on deck, but pushed the questions away. If she wanted to tell him, she'd tell him.

She handed him the soup bowl, followed by a hunk of bread. Missing hand aside, his left arm was healing steadily, and he'd regained enough strength to sit up on his own. He'd even been working on standing, taking small careful steps around the room, as far as the chains would allow him, when he was sure he was alone. Feeble preparations for an escape opportunity that may never present itself, but each footfall was a small victory, proving to himself that whatever torments Peter dreamt up, he could still stand tall.

The soup of the day was thicker than usual, a hearty mash of beans and bacon. It was probably the best meal he'd had in weeks, and though he did his best to eat slowly, his attempts to savor it didn't last long.

Jeddy said nothing as he ate, which was far from unusual, but something in her gaze weighed heavier today. Hesitant. Regretful.

James gave up on his earlier resolve not to question her.

"Jeddy? What's the matter?" The words came out strangely slurred, his vision wavering as he raised his head to look at her.

Was ... was he getting sick again? But what would be the cause? His thoughts strung together lazily, hardly making sense.

He *couldn't* be sick. There was no plague aboard the ship, and ... no.

No.

He grasped the bowl, clumsy fingers already half-numbed. The scant remains of the soup coating the curved wooden edges of the dish shimmered as they caught the dim light, reflecting back in shining greens and blues.

Sailors called it scale. It was said to be made from mermaid tail and the skin of fish from the southern seas, but for all its supposed rarity, it had no problem circulating the waters, clouding minds, turning men to addiction.

"No," he said aloud, and the word came up garbled, distantly furious that the drug had even found its way aboard his ship. Who'd brought it on? How had Jeddy known? The anger quickly dissolved as a pleasantly cool feeling began to spread through his core, leaching into his limbs.

"Sorry capt – 'M sorry," Jeddy was saying, her figure shifting like a mirage as the walls of the room seemed to warp and melt around her.

His mind felt fuzzy, his thoughts seemed to shimmer before his eyes. The pain – in his arm, his joints, his stomach – was *gone*, replaced by a dizzy giddiness, and he almost laughed in relief.

Maybe he did laugh in relief. It was hard to tell.

Jeddy was standing up, walking or sliding or floating toward the door. He was angry with her. Was he? Why was he?

It was nice, *good*, to not feel the ache, the hunger. To not be afraid. Why *had* he been afraid in the first place? He was on his ship. He was *home*. It was good.

Jeddy was looking down at him, and she was so very far away, yet he could see every detail of her face. An impassive expression betrayed by tears that streamed like black oil. He couldn't tell if they were real or just another product of the scale.

"Peter's comin'," she said as she seized the door handle, and her voice grew, echoed, doubled and doubled until it was like a rhythm in his head.

Peter's comin'.
Peter's comin'.

5

COMPASS ROSE

James felt like he was underwater.

Everything was muffled. Sound, sight, feeling, all dampened by the flow that consumed him. It was like floating facedown, staring at the ocean floor, but somehow still being able to breathe. The room around him distorted and rippled as if each plank of wood was being pulled by the tide, each bit of scant light dancing with the motion of the waves.

It was beautiful.

He couldn't remember the last time he'd felt so content, so *peaceful*. If he'd ever felt that way at all, unbothered by the pitch and roll of the world, it would have been when he was very young. A child, unaware of the kings and governors who would dictate his life, of the ships he would flee to in order to be free, of the weight of responsibility that would settle on his shoulders in time. In that moment, nothing mattered. Nothing, save the feeling of floating and the shifting shape of the room.

Peter swam in eventually, a funny-looking fish if there ever was one. James almost laughed at the notion. But when Peter came, he brought the fear along with him, trailing behind like a shadow, laughing all the way up to where James lay, though his face was unmoving. Was Peter cheerful or angry? James couldn't tell. Both were equally bad, he knew, but his dread felt like a whisper. Drowned out by the waves all around him.

Peter said something, but he was too far away to hear. James felt his arms being lifted, folded together and placed above his head. Peter produced a rope and began weaving it around his wrists, his forearms, his elbows, binding it tighter and tighter until James's shoulders were straining. It *burned*, but was swiftly cooled by the water around him, and he found himself relaxing in spite of the distant ache.

Peter drew his knife, the little polished crocodile that had taken his hand, and a spike of fear shot through him like a rock tossed into a pool. Was the monster here for his other hand or would it devour something new today? James tried to move away, but his body wouldn't listen. Panic washed over him, but the cool peacefulness pushed back. Ebb and flow. Push and pull. His body grew cooler still as Peter tossed aside the blanket that covered his legs and held the sharp-mouthed reptile to his chest, letting its teeth cut through his shirt before pushing back the fabric to better expose his bare torso.

James's heart thrummed in time with the waves as the other man traced down his ribcage with the tip of the knife. Peter's smile seemed to surround him. No matter where he looked, he couldn't escape it.

"We're in uncharted waters now, James," Peter said. "We're almost there."

Almost there. Almost where? He couldn't make sense of any of the words. *Almost to shore, almost to port, almost to the bottom of the sea to raid sunken cities.*

The knife rested on his sternum for a moment, then moved down over his abdomen, his navel, crossing his waist and coming back up.

"I found it on a map, you know," Peter said. "An old map. A *treasure* map. I was overjoyed. I wanted to show you, but then you'd know. And you couldn't know, not if I wanted the ship."

James opened his mouth to ask what Peter meant, but words wouldn't form. No more than a groan came out, and Peter hushed him.

"But now I *have* the ship," Peter said, pressing a finger to his lips. "And I have *you*. And I'm very excited to show you my map."

The knifepoint – tooth of the crocodile – slid down to balance on his hip, gentle as a pinprick for all of a second before Peter began pressing down. James was vaguely aware of pain blooming as the little golden monster bit into him, of the resulting blood trickling down his side. He flinched as Peter dragged the knife into his flesh, pulled it out, and crossed the mark with another line.

"This is where we are," Peter said. "Or at least our general direction. This..." he brought the knife up, placed it over James' sternum – no, his *heart* – and cut another X. "This is where we're going."

He smiled as James writhed, trying to escape the crocodile's bite.

"But of course, our destination is inland," Peter said. "Now hold still."

James probably screamed. It was hard to tell under the effects of the scale. He certainly *felt* like screaming, as Peter dug the knife into his side, under his collarbone, across one shoulder. Tracing out the ridges of a land mass.

"There's said to be mountains surrounding it," Peter said, carving jagged lines across his chest. "A smaller island too. We'll be sailing around that." A wavering circle cut into the skin over his stomach. "We'll dock in a cove here." An angled cut into the right side of his ribcage. "The path of travel is fairly straightforward ... " A dashed line, crossing his torso, connecting one X to the other. "And we can't forget to give you a compass rose." Meticulously carved into his left hip; a hot coal plunged into the waters James was floating in, sinking to settle on his flesh.

He tried to remember how to *breathe*, doing his damndest to keep his eyes on the ceiling, not on the dead-eyed knife, not on the bloody ruin of his chest.

It had been nearly bearable at first, with the scale granting him distance from the pain. But now the biting sharpness was starting to draw nearer. James didn't know if the effects of the drug were already wearing off or if it was all the doing of Peter's knife. He could only gasp like a fish pulled from the water as the feeling sharpened, Peter's map radiating agony with every breath.

The other man stood, surveying his handiwork, and James thought it might be over. Blood ran freely down his chest, soaking into his pants, pooling on the mat, and all he wanted to do was curl in on himself. Hide under the blanket and try to sleep, try to sink back into the cool, calming waters, just for a little while.

He was becoming aware of other pains again. His shoulders burned from the strained position his arms had been bound in, and his throat felt ragged. An ache had begun in his temple, like there was ice forming on the inside of his skull, and he squeezed his eyes shut in a bid to relieve the pressure.

When he opened them, Peter had knelt back down. Knife in hand.

"See? Now we each have a map," he said, his blade hovering over the first X, the one on James's hip. The blood there had begun to clot. "And I'm going to make certain that yours doesn't fade."

James knew it was coming before the knifepoint touched him.

"No, no, n – *AUGHH!*"

It dug in as deeply as before, piercing the already-damaged skin. Without much pause, Peter repeated the process with the X over his heart. James tried to force himself to breathe, though he already felt dizzy. He could only hope he was rendered unconscious soon.

Because Peter still had the mainland. The mountains. The island. The cove. The path of travel. And the compass rose.

6

— · —

CHANCE

James faded into unconsciousness halfway through the mainland's retracing and awoke shivering, a headache brought on by the drug's aftereffects sitting frigid in his skull.

He was still bound tight, unable to move for fear of dislocating his shoulders, with the ache there steadily growing into an agony he couldn't ignore. It almost rivaled that of his torso. The bloody map had dried. A mess of blacks and browns and reds covered his chest and abdomen. He hardly dared to *breathe* for fear of reopening the wounds.

Jeddy made her appearance some time later, when the layers of pain over pain had become almost unbearable, and he'd fallen to quiet whimpering. She cut the ropes first, slowly uncurling his arms, placing them down at his sides when he couldn't move them himself, then began to clean the cuts. She wouldn't meet his eyes.

James wanted to yell, to ask her what in the seven hells gave her the *right*, ask her if she realized she'd taken away one of his last freedoms, that she'd taken the sanctity of his own *mind*, but he didn't.

He didn't have the energy. And perhaps more than that, he didn't want to risk driving away the one person who was showing him any kindness, no matter how misguided.

Well-intentioned betrayal was still betrayal.

He sucked in air through gritted teeth as she washed the wounds on his chest. Gentle as she tried to be, there was no way to make such a thing painless, and he could either suffer through it or die of gangrene when the wounds soured.

She'd brought two bowls for the wound tending. The first was warm water. The second ... Though he knew it was necessary, his stomach roiled as Jeddy dipped a cloth into it. She looked down at him for all of an instant, a silent apology on her face as she brought the brandy-soaked rag toward his hips. James only nodded, clenched his jaw, squeezed his eyes shut. It was like being set ablaze, like the map was being retraced a third time in acrid, stinging flames.

When it was done, when he lay there shaking, Jeddy gathered the supplies and left. She came back moments later, another bowl in hand. Knelt by him. Offered a spoonful of soup like there was nothing *wrong* –

"No," he said. "I – I can't."

"You're gonna have to eat somethin'," she said. "This one ... this one's fine. Nothin' hidden in it."

"I thought the same of the last one," James said, eyeing the bowl, looking for the telltale shine of the drug. But it didn't have to be scale, did it? She could do the same with another substance, perhaps something he'd never even heard of.

"It's not. I swear it."

"How do I know you're being truthful? Where did you *get* it? I don't allow scale on *my ship.*" His voice rose, sharpened by the sting of the cuts, and she bowed her head.

"I *am* sorry for it. I only wanted to help. The last time almost killed you, and – "

"I understand that, but I said *no*. Jeddy, I told you not to. How do I know you won't go against my wishes again?"

"You – " She sighed. "You'd rather starve then? Rather than risk it?"

Yes. No. *He didn't know*. Denying any food would take away the chance of escape just as quickly as giving himself up to the scale, but that wasn't the point. He already felt so helpless here, to the point that refusing a meal was one of the few things he had any power over. No matter how he pleaded, he couldn't stop Jeddy from drugging him again. The choice really *was* to give in to the possibility or starve, but how many more times could he consume the drug before it consumed *him*, before he was lost anyway?

The silence between them was broken as Jeddy suddenly seized the spoon, plunging it into the bowl and taking a bite herself.

"There. There, how about now? Will you eat?" she said, pushing the spoon back into his hand. The way his head was swimming, it took a moment to understand what she'd done, to fully grasp the display, the assurance that he could trust her, at least this time.

James nodded, his fingers curling around the utensil's handle.

"I'm sorry for it. I am," she said.

"No more," James said. "Not again. Whatever Peter does ... whatever piece of me he decides to cut apart or break, I can take it."

"Not again," she agreed, and he could tell that she meant it.

***

Peter came up with a new torment in the week that followed, one that didn't require him to lift even a finger. Beatings.

Men who had been a part of his crew not even a month prior would throw the door open to beat the living daylights out of James, opening his wounds, leaving him groaning and gasping for breath. The bursts of violence never lasted long – Peter didn't necessarily want him *dead*, after all – but they came unannounced, never at the same hour twice. Morning, noon, or night, he couldn't anticipate their arrival. He couldn't run either. Couldn't fight back. Could barely do more than lie there and attempt to shield himself.

The first time, he'd thought it was Jeddy opening the door, only to be met with two of the brutes who worked the sails, barely giving him time to register what was happening before a kick to his stomach had him curled into a ball, waiting for the blows to end.

That seemed to be his stance on life lately: close his eyes and hope it would be over soon. The only pleasant thing he could scrounge from this new situation was that he hadn't seen Peter in days. Jeddy still made her rounds, thankfully, often coming by right after the men left to clean up whatever mess they'd made of him.

James gave up on taking the beatings stoically after the first four or five or six times. What good was pride anymore, except as a drain on the little energy he had? He'd whimper, he'd cry, he'd beg for it to *stop*, but he'd spite them all by continuing to live.

Injuries have a tendency to layer on each other, James mused as he stared at the wall, cheek laid on the cool wooden floor. Was it that? Or had they just been particularly vicious this time? It was difficult to tell. One blow tended to merge with the next, and it wasn't as if he were counting them all.

How many times would Peter send them in? How much more could he take before he lost himself completely, before he became a shadow of a man? It already felt like he was on the verge of giving up. Of begging Peter to *just kill him already*. Of asking Jeddy for the scale after all. Anything to escape the pain he lived in.

He coughed, the movement turning into a wince as pain spiked through his ribs. The half-healed map Peter had cut into his chest throbbed where boots had come into contact with the careful red lines. His right eye was all but swollen shut, and he was almost certain some of his teeth had broken but was too tired to even poke around with his tongue and find out. Everything hurt, the combination of exhaustion and pain heavy enough that he could lie in the muddle, half-conscious, and pretend he felt nothing at all.

The sharp inhale Jeddy made when she swung the door open was enough to tell him that he looked as bad as he felt. She knelt next to him, warm brown hand coming down to rest on his shoulder, the only kind touch he could hope for anymore.

"Are you ... are you awake?"

James wanted to say yes, but all that came from his throat was a pitiful whine. She grimaced, then set about cleaning the cuts on his abdomen. There wasn't much else she *could* do. The only true medicine for him was rest, and he wasn't about to hold out hope for that.

"I can't stop them," Jeddy said as she washed the wounds. "I wish I could. Ain't right, beatin' a bound man. But they do as Peter says, and even if I were able to knock 'em back, he'd only send more."

"Would ... " James cringed, sucked in air, forced out the words. "Would *you*? If Peter ordered you to, would you ... " He let the question trail off, not wanting to even bring the words into existence. *Would you hurt me? Would you add to my torment on an order?*

She pressed her lips together, not answering at first.

Did he want her to? If she said yes, or worse, if she said *no* only for her actions to speak otherwise, would he have anything left but despair? In this state, he had no chance of escape. If he could hold out, if Peter got bored but left him alive, there was a *chance*, but that couldn't happen if he didn't have someone who cared at least a little. Enough to bring him food. Enough to tend his wounds, even in the dead of night. He couldn't bear the thought of losing Jeddy, of her gentle touch turning to harm. The sole ill she'd brought upon him was the scale, and even that had been done with good intent.

"I don't know," Jeddy said at last. "The *Merry*'s my home, I can't leave her. But ... " Her eyes trailed over his body. The bruises and weeping cuts that clouded his flesh, the remains of his left arm. "But I can't hurt you neither."

Something in him – a twist of anxiety in his gut that he hadn't noticed until now – uncurled, sending a feeling of relief sweeping over him. One person still cared whether he lived or died. And that was enough, *had to be* enough.

"Thank you." The words were a whisper. He wasn't lost, not just yet. It would take luck and a lot of holding on, but there was still a chance.

He still had a chance.

7

— ⋅ —

IN ALL OF HER GLORY

For a few days, James was granted a reprieve. No blows, no Peter, just stew and rest.

A brief period to heal, likely so his captor could send some new torture crashing onto him, but James refused to look a gift horse in the mouth. He was alive. For a day, and then another, he was alive.

He spent most of his time asleep, his body struggling to recover. On Jeddy's third visit since his last beating, James was able to sit up again, to feed himself again. Wounds began to seal themselves, bruises yellowing and clotted cuts turning to scabs with fading edges. Strength seeped into him like sunlight pushing its rays through an overcast sky, and James did his best to savor it. He did not want to think of the storm on the horizon.

The day the clouds blackened came all too soon. Peter's men tramped down to the brig with a footfall that rumbled like thunder. James curled up at the sound, awaiting the pain he was certain they'd bring. But this time, no blows followed the creaking of the door, only hands that held him in place as his chains rattled and the manacles that bound him fell away. They were taking him from the brig.

The notion of leaving the room, of breathing sunlight and clean air, should've been a joyous one, but it was weighed down by a sudden dread. They wouldn't take him above deck without reason. *What did Peter want?*

His body was stiff, his legs refusing to support him as he was dragged up the narrow wooden staircase. James's heart pounded as they grew closer to daylight, closer to whatever cruelty Peter had laid out for him. Perhaps the day had at last arrived for James to die. Perhaps Peter wished to be rid of him once and for all.

The thought of death was softer than James had imagined it would be; a simple end to the torment, a stop in the path. Hope was a draining thing, death was rest. Knowing Peter, the treacherous man would drag it out, turn it into a nightmarish spectacle, but then it would be over. What followed the end was a mystery, but surely it was a kinder unknown than the one he would face if he lived.

Jeddy entered his thoughts then, sudden as a gale, and a feeling akin to guilt washed over him. And why? This was *his* life, *his* torment, had he not the right to wish for an end to it? Why did welcoming the reaper feel like spitting in her face?

She wanted him to live. She had hope. Perhaps that was why it felt wrong to lose his grip on his own so quickly.

James was nearly blinded as they reached the deck, sunlight touching him for the first time in weeks. He blinked away the light, trying to savor its warmth as he waited for his eyes to adjust to the shift. Once they did, he allowed himself to forget his sorry lot for just a moment as he looked around, taking in *The Scarlet Merry*.

To Peter's credit, she was still in top shape, deck practically gleaming, blazing red sails standing out beautifully against a blue sky. If he were to die today, at least he could see her in all of her glory one last time.

The water surrounding the ship was a fine turquoise. Far ahead, he could see a mountain range that seemed to rise out of the sea, and just ahead of that, a smaller island that seemed to have more rock than shore.

The cuts on his chest throbbed.

They'd made it. Peter's island.

"Welcome back!"

And there was Peter himself, cheery as ever, the sun gleaming in his auburn hair. He let out a sharp whistle, and the sailors around them ceased their work, coming to stand in a half-circle around James.

Weeks ago, he might've called them together in a similar manner, to plot a raid or divvy up loot. Weeks ago, he'd not an inkling it would ever come to this. He doubted he much resembled the man they'd once called captain. Beaten, starved, cut to pieces, in too much pain to stand unassisted.

James tried to keep his head held high, eyes fixed on the horizon, pretending they weren't there. Pretending it *was* weeks ago, and he was still the captain, still someone they held in respect. Pretending they'd never had to listen to his *screams*.

"Now, don't look so *morose*, James. Haven't you missed your old crew?" Peter called out, striding into the circle to face him. James met his eyes, only his eyes. He didn't need to acknowledge anyone else, didn't want to see what shame or pity or *apathy* rested on their faces.

"Well?" Peter gestured widely, spreading his arms in the direction of the distant shore. "What did I tell you? Almost there. Exciting, isn't it?"

James inhaled, exhaled slowly, let the quiet grow for a moment. "Is that why I'm up here, Peter? To see your island?"

"Yes. Well, partly." He walked around to stand behind James, prompting a flinch as he set his hands on his shoulders. "I thought you might be lonely. Life's a little dull when you're on your own down below, hm?" He began to apply pressure, maneuvering James into a kneel. James tried to keep his breathing even as dread seeped in, choking his thoughts, making it difficult to think about anything but what came next, what new idea Peter had for him.

"I think we should play another game or two, don't you?" Peter said when the silence dragged on too long.

Of course. What purpose did James serve anymore, besides amusing a sadistic man? Why should he hope for anything besides pain when Peter decided to show his face? The other man moved back around, smiling down at James for a long moment, staring like a child about to pull the wings off an insect.

"Can I cut off your hand?"

The tension snapped like a twig, a consuming wave of nausea and panic surging through James as he looked right through his former first mate, staring at nothing as he tried to remember how to *breathe.*

No, no, no, he couldn't. Not again, he *couldn't.*

He was looking away from Peter, he was facing the deck, he was *falling*, he was being hauled back to his knees by the two men on either side of him, blood rushing in his ears.

He was below again, tied up. He was trying not to look as Peter dug out another joint, started flaying another strip of flesh, made the first cut.

"James," Peter said, his voice singsong. "I asked you a question."

"*No –* "

"No? So you want it to be an especially *long* game like last time – "

"Please. Please, don't ... " He drew a shaky breath that didn't quite reach his lungs, the words spilling out like blood from a cut throat. He was aware of the stares from the crew. Pity. Horror. Disgust. He didn't care, couldn't care, *couldn't breathe.*

"*Please* don't, please no, not *again*, *please.*"

"Aw, James, you're confusing me. You don't want me to cut it off? Or you don't want to play the game?"

"D-don't ... th-the game." He barely got the words out.

Peter's smile widened. "So you do want me to cut it off then?"

"Yes."

"Say it."

"C-cut it off. *Please* just – just cut it off."

"What a shame," Peter shook his head. "I wanted to try and get more pieces this time. Maybe saw through a bone. Scoop out the marrow. Are you *sure*?"

James could only nod, frantic, tears streaming down his face. "Please. *Please.* I don't – I *can't* – just cut it off. Please."

For a while, there was nothing. James could see nothing but the *Merry*'s deck, blurred with tears, his heartbeat pounding in his head like a gallows drummer.

Then Peter began to laugh.

"Why, James, I was only joking," he said, leaning down to ruffle his hair. "We've already played *that* game."

James slowly began to lift his head, his body still shaking, choked sobs still wracking his chest, painfully shifting his bruised ribs.

It was a joke. *It was a joke.*

He could taste his relief.

"I'd still like to do *something,* though," Peter continued, but James didn't care.

Anything. Anything but *that*.

For the first time, as if emboldened by his escape from the knife, his gaze reached past Peter to take in his former crew.

Cotts, the boatswain.

Fiver, the cook.

Jeddy.

Not a single sailor was looking at him. Grim expressions fixed on the deck, the bow, the sea. They didn't want to see this, didn't want to watch Peter's cruelties play out. But no one moved to stop it either.

He allowed his head to drop once more. Peter crouched in front of him.

"As fun as it was to watch you snivel, I think I'm ready for the next part now," he said politely. From his belt, he drew the polished little dagger, the dead-eyed devouring *beast*. Set it on the deck before James. Stood for a moment, and was handed something else, which he laid next to the knife.

It was a coiled whip. A cat-o'-nine-tails, the lead at the end of each thin leather braid glinting in the sunlight.

Peter tapped a boot before the items. "I want you to choose," he said. "I want *you* to pick what you want to happen next."

James swallowed, his gaze darting back and forth.

Whip. Knife. Whip. Knife.

Each implement spoke of pain, but the sharpest of his fear had bled away with the threat against his hand. It had been replaced by a numb distance, the sort that used to settle onto him when he was poring over maps by candlelight, wits dulled by lack of sleep. He regarded the items before him with the same eyes that would stare at strait and landmass, tiredly seeking the smoothest course.

A flogging would be brutal. A flogging could drag away what little life he had left in him. But the knife held uncertainty.

What would Peter do if he chose the knife? Cut off something else? Make good on his threat to take his eye? Carve another picture into his back?

A flogging would be bad, yes, but at least he knew what would happen if he chose the whip. A flogging was better than losing an eye.

A flogging was better than the painstaking removal of his remaining hand.

With a shaking finger, he pointed to the whip.

"That one, huh?" Peter said. "It's nice to know what you want, James. It really is. Makes things more fun if you participate, right?"

He stood up and wordlessly walked into the crowd of sailors. It wasn't the end of it. James knew by now that it was always more than threats. There was always something coming.

Peter came back, not a minute later, Jeddy following after him. He gestured down at the items.

Knife. Whip.

James was frozen in place, dread bubbling up all over again as he tried to keep his jaw rigid, tried not to cry.

"How about you, Esme?" Peter asked Jeddy. Her eyes were downcast. Her face stony. "What game should we play with our dear friend James?"

8

— · —

HIS OWN SHIP

She chose the knife.

One of the men holding James clamped a hand over his mouth on Peter's orders, so he couldn't sway her decision. And she chose the knife. He let out a muffled cry as Peter picked up the blade and pressed it into Jeddy's hand. *Not her, not her.*

"Are you an artist, Esme?"

"No, sir." Her voice was flat. Emotionless.

"What about writing then, do you know your letters?"

"I do, sir."

Peter left her standing there and wrenched James's right arm away from his side.

"Hold him down."

James was forced onto his stomach, one of the men digging a knee into his back. He cried out at the sudden pressure on his ribs. Peter's fingers tightened around his wrist, pulling until his meager strength was overcome and his arm was forcibly straightened. Peter knelt on his palm, his weight driving James's knuckles into the unyielding wood of the deck. One hand remained on his wrist, further ensuring the arm would not move.

"There we are," he said. "Now, Esme, I'd like you to write your name."

"My name, sir?" Her voice was like still water, a careful surface seeking to appease a ship's captain.

"Yes." He smiled. "I want you to carve it into his arm."

James thrashed, though he knew it was pointless. Peter held the power here. He could do whatever he wanted, including shatter one of his few remaining solaces.

The stillness shielding Jeddy seemed to ripple, and she staggered back a half step. "Sir, I-I can't."

"I'm sure you'll find that you can," Peter said. The pressure on James's hand let up for a moment as he stood, clapping Jeddy on the shoulder in a gesture that mocked friendliness. Encouragement. "Now, go on."

Another of Peter's brutes took his place, seizing James's arm and holding it against the deck. From the furthest corner of his vision, he could see Jeddy's face, nothing to betray her feelings but a slight crease between her brows.

"Sir – " She stopped short as Peter leaned in.

"It's going to be either your name or mine, Esme. And only one of those choices ends with you still onboard. Do you understand?"

Jeddy's jaw tightened. "I ... I understand."

She knelt beside James, as she'd often done before. Only this time she wasn't helping him to eat or drink, wasn't cleaning a fresh wound, all soft touch and soothing words. This time, she was the one who wielded the knife.

He understood, he *told himself* he understood, though his chest hitched and he squirmed under the weight of the men in a weak attempt to get away.

It would happen either way.

It would happen either way, and at least this way, only one person had to hurt. Only him. *But why did it have to be her?*

Her hand came to rest on his forearm, palm warm and familiar. A part of James wanted to relax under her touch, for how many times had she steadied him to dab at a cut? But in her other hand, she held Peter's hungry little beast, not linen scraps. The point of the blade pricked against the soft skin of his forearm and she pressed in, making the first line –

"Deeper," Peter said. "Or it won't scar right."

Jeddy nodded, silent as ever, and James tried to hold back from making any sounds, more for her sake than his.

Compared to Peter's other ideas, this is tame, he told himself. It wasn't his hand, it wasn't a terrible pain. He would be alright, he'd suffered worse in the days behind him.

But no matter how he tried to insist it was so, he knew it wasn't about the pain. Jeddy had been the one to nurse him through the worst. To see her on the other side threatened to break something in him. He could hide from the truth, he could pretend it wasn't her doing the damage, pretend it was only Peter –

"James, open your eyes if you'd like to keep them."

And so he did, a gasp escaping him as she began a second line. A third, a fourth. A bloody 'E' cut into his wrist.

The shine of tears in her eyes was the only thing that betrayed her neutral expression. The sight of them stirred a mixture of feelings within him. A great relief that she did not want this, that all her weeks of care *were* care, not simply following orders. A greater sorrow for her own pain. And under them both, speaking to him with a liar's tongue, betrayal. It wasn't her fault. Here, she had no choice, but he couldn't silence the sick insistence.

If Peter ordered you to, would you?

He breathed through each slice as best he could, unable to look away as she carved each crimson letter, the razored teeth of the knife almost gentle in her hands.

E-S-M-E

He wanted to tell her it was alright. That he could not blame her for the obedience that kept her safe, but he couldn't open his mouth. Couldn't form the words.

She stopped after that, bloodied knife laid on the deck beside her, hands clasped in her lap. Head down, eyes not meeting his. Peter said nothing as he knelt to examine James's arm. It hung limp as he seized the wrist and lifted it, angling it this way and that as if to let the new wound catch the sunlight. He let go of it suddenly, allowing the limb to fall back onto the deck.

"I don't like it," he said.

"Cut it off," he said.

Cut it off. The skin or the hand or the arm? What did he mean? Would she obey?

The image came to his mind, Jeddy gently sawing through his wrist with that same stony expression, eyes glistening even as her hands held him down, sliding the knife back and forth and back and forth until it slid through his skin. It was all he could do to hold back a sob.

"Captain ... " Her voice was quiet, the single word sounding like a plea. Who was it for? For Peter to show mercy? For James to forgive her?

"*Esme,*" Peter replied in the same tone. "Will you do it?"

She shook her head, and Peter clicked his tongue, bending down to pick up the bloodied knife. He wiped the beast's scarlet mouth on his pants and tucked the blade into his belt.

"That's alright," he said, then bent down to take the whip in hand. Letting it uncoil as he stood.

"It's time for James's pick anyway."

***

He'd felt the bite of the whip once, years before his days aboard the *Merry*, and though it hurt, the welts had healed swiftly, having not even broken skin.

But that had been only five lashes, and not from a cat-o'-nine.

James didn't struggle as they bound him to the mainmast, the rope digging into the fresh cuts on his forearm. He could not dredge up the energy to feel frustrated at the trick, and even if he could, there was no point in wasting it. Peter had known what he wanted from the start. No matter the choice James or Jeddy made, he'd been destined for both torments the moment he was dragged onto the deck.

James tried to keep his breathing deep and steady, though it was difficult with the tension on his torso. Breathe through the pain, through the dread, through the knowledge that this could be the end. He closed his eyes, not wanting to see his former crew standing around him, waiting for the spectacle to begin; not wanting to look back and see whether it was Peter or Jeddy or some other crewmember who would be the one to swing the whip.

He could hear it drag behind him, lead bits scraping along the wooden deck as it drew nearer.

"Do you want to hear the rules of this game, James?" Peter's voice came from a few feet over his shoulder. "Because if you win ... " He trailed off. "If you win, I'll let you go."

Let him go. James would've laughed had he the breath to spare. Let him go *now*, shamed and broken. If Peter meant it in earnest, did that mean he'd be dropped at the nearest port, to die of gangrene or starvation when he could not find work? Or did Peter mean it in a literal sense, to be released from the *Merry*, to sink to the bottom of the sea?

Of the two, the ocean seemed the kinder fate. A soft ending in the arms of the one who had carried him so long.

"Well?" Peter said, and his voice was a step behind him. "Aren't you going to ask what the rules are?"

"Wh ... what are the rules?" James mumbled, resting his forehead against the mast. His arms were already beginning to lose feeling from being strung up. Perhaps it was a mercy; one less layer of pain.

"If you can stay awake through a certain number of strikes, you're free. Doesn't that sound fun? *Free*." Peter leaned in close to murmur in his ear. "So, how many will it be, James? How many do you think you'll make it through?"

Free, free to be drowned or abandoned, and yet it was still better than his own ship, the home that had turned into a hell. James knew Peter's play. Too low and he would laugh afterwards, say he didn't quite *earn* his freedom, condemn him to weeks more of torturous *games*. Too high, and his body wouldn't stand a chance against the whip. If Peter was feeling particularly cruel, he'd call any number too low, forcing him to raise the count until he bled out right here. An ending, an avoidance of further torment, and yet he found his spirit rebelled at the thought. If he were to die, it could not be here, it could not be to Peter. Surrendering to the sea felt more like a choice; even being abandoned at a foreign port left his fate in his own hands. He would not die strung up like an animal.

"Ten," he said through gritted teeth, hoping it was enough to satisfy Peter, enough to let him survive for just a little longer.

"*Ten*," the other man repeated, sounding surprised. "I would've wagered five! But I like your pluck. Ten it is."

James's heart sank. Chances were, Peter would say that no matter what he chose, but it still felt like he'd duped himself. *Ten.* More blood from him to be stolen, but perhaps it could be the last. Perhaps after this, he'd never have to look up on Peter's cruel smile again.

"Let's begin."

The whip came down, its whistle through the air the only warning before the first strike. It hit right in the center of James's back, pain spiking through his body with the brightness of lightning. He didn't even have time to cry out before the next one followed it, striking him in the side, lead tips colliding with his bruised ribs, and this time he *did* scream, a horrible, ragged sound.

A third. His head was already swimming, and he clenched his jaw. Seven more. Such a small number and yet it may as well be infinite.

"Hh – *Aughh*!" Four.

Five. His vision was splotched with white. *Stay awake. See it through.*

"Halfway," Peter sang out. "And just think, that could've been the last one if you weren't so *ambitious*."

The sixth came down, dragging out another hoarse scream.

Seven.

Eight.

His vision was fading in and out, his body shaking with pain and fatigue. *Hold on. Just hold on.*

Nine. His back had been set ablaze, lines of fire carved in his skin, spreading, reaching up to take him ...

Ten. His body jerked under the final stroke, the only sound escaping him a choked whine. Over. It was over it was over it was over. He was conscious only by the most base definition, seeing but not aware, hearing but not understanding. Feeling the pain roll through him like the tide. Nearly unbearable, threatening to smother him, *drown him*, but he fought it, no matter how much he wanted to sink beneath its waves and cease to know the world around him.

"Well done!" Peter's voice rang around him. "Didn't think you had it in you."

Hands reached up, cut the ropes, let his body hit the deck limply, his eyes staring emptily at the horizon.

"You've impressed me, James." Peter and his smile were over him, silhouetted in blue. "I think you deserve more than freedom. I think you may even deserve to be captain again."

Captain? James thought, the word spinning in his head. No, no, that was nonsense. Peter would never step down. He wouldn't allow things to be as they were, and even if he did, nothing would ever be the same. James couldn't leave behind the last weeks, couldn't bury it all. His hand would never return to him, and the wounds inflicted by knife and whip would plague him the rest of his days. What sort of captain could he be, in this body Peter had twisted to his whims? Even if he were to undo every injury, his crew would never forget how he'd groveled and begged after one whispered threat. He was no longer *fit* to be captain.

"What do you think? Captain of your own ship again."

Of his own ship.

James winced as Peter grabbed him by the hair, lifted his head just enough so he could see the crowd part for a pair of men carrying a large barrel. It took him a moment to truly see it, and another to comprehend it. He took in the broomstick tied to the barrel, a mockery of a mast, the bit of canvas that stood for a sail.

"Beautiful, isn't she? About to take her maiden voyage." Peter released James, and his head dropped.

He'd been brought up to die after all. A mocking death to be sure, but it would end with him wrapped in the waves, sinking under, never to be touched by Peter again, never to shrink from the gleam of his knife. He let his eyes drift closed. Let them throw him overboard, let them have it over with.

"And what's a captain without a first mate?"

His eyes flew open, and with all his remaining strength, he lifted his head to see the crowd make way once more, heads hung, eyes downcast.

Jeddy was brought forward, one of Peter's brutes on either side of her, tearstains on her cheeks.

"S-sir, I don't – "

"You don't what?" Peter said, and his voice was measured. Cool. "You don't think I know everything that happens on my ship? You don't think I know the signs of scale use?"

No ...

"You've shown yourself to be a liar and a coward," Peter said, his voice rising. Not in anger, nor in indignation, but in something that resembled theatrics. It was nearly jovial. It was all just a show for him; one more game.

"I gave you the chance to redeem yourself, to prove your loyalty, but you threw it away. You have no place on this ship."

Jeddy's shoulders shook. "Please. Captain. Don't make me leave her."

"Leave her?" Peter folded his arms. "You ought to count yourself lucky I didn't throw you in the *brig* when I found out."

"Peter ... " James's voice came out, more whimper than word. "L-leave her be."

The other man shook his head, putting a hand on Jeddy's shoulder in such a way that it almost looked friendly. The false anger had drained from his face, replaced with his careless grin. "Don't tell me how to run my ship. You can call the shots once you're aboard your own," he said with a wink, waving on the men with the barrel.

"Now *heave-ho*, boys. We have a ship to launch."

9

— · —

MANY TIMES OVER

Peter at least had the courtesy to throw the barrel overboard first.

James was quick to follow it, hands lifting him up, rolling him over the side, letting him fall into the waiting arms of the sea.

He must've blacked out when he hit the water, salt burning into the whip marks with such a fury it shut his mind down. He was screaming when the black had faded, screaming into the brine, drawing in no air, just the salt, just the *sea*. He couldn't tell which direction would lead him to the surface, but he knew he was sinking, and even the primal creature within him that still sought to survive couldn't find the energy to fight the pull of the deep.

An arm curled around his waist before the black could claim him again, lean and strong, hauling him through the waves until his head broke into air, and he was choking, coughing up seawater, his back feeling like it was *blistering*, though the water was cold.

Jeddy.

She seized the barrel by the rope twisted around it and wound it around his arms in such a way it would keep his head above the water when she released her grip on him.

Far above, on the deck of *The Scarlet Merry*, James could hear laughter, hear Peter saying something but couldn't focus on the words.

He closed his eyes.

Just for a moment, he thought, but when he opened them again, the *Merry* was a silhouette on the horizon, set aglow by the setting sun. Jeddy's arms were on either side of him and she was kicking into the waves, guiding them toward the rocky little shore that stood between them and Peter's island.

James watched it grow closer, little by little, with vision that was hazy and blurred. He couldn't tell how far they had to go, didn't know how long he'd been in the water, only that he was dizzy and cold and *weak*.

Shadows cast by the dying sun gave the rock face the appearance of a grinning skull.

How fitting, James thought, before allowing himself to slip back into the calm unknowing of unconsciousness.

***

When he awoke, the side of his face was pressed into the sand and his legs were being lapped at by a gentle tide. James shivered, trying to lift his head and look around, not even making it an *inch* before giving up.

Where was Jeddy?

His head pounded, his back was numb, his body leaden. All he wanted to do was sink back into sleep, but he knew if he let that happen, he would never wake. The thought should've filled him with peace, but instead it only brought dread. *Not yet*, pleaded a voice within him, *not yet.*

James shifted his right arm, moving it up bit by bit until his fingertips were in line with his eyes. He grit his teeth and tried to lift his head again, this time with an arm to support him. It took far more effort than it should've, but he managed, turning his head to look down the other side of the shore. And there she was.

Her knees were tucked into her chest, arms hugging them tightly, eyes fixed on the horizon. The barrel that had carried them here sat a few feet behind her. She had to be exhausted, but her back was too straight for her to be asleep.

She was grieving, James knew. The loss of a ship, of a *home.* For him, leaving the *Merry* meant escaping Peter and the tortures he dreamt up, but what had Jeddy escaped? She was here because of him. She'd lost *everything* for him, and she deserved a chance to mourn that.

But right now he was sure he was dying and could barely even lift his head. He'd need her help once more, despite having taken so much of it already.

"J ... eddy," he croaked, his voice hoarse from thirst, from screaming, from swallowing seawater. She gave no sign she'd heard him.

"Please," he tried again. "Please ... Jeddy," and the words took so much *effort*, but she moved. She pushed herself up from the sand, her expression serious as ever, though there were tears drying on her cheeks. Soon he was being rolled onto his back and lifted, the pressure on the scourge marks cutting through the numbness he felt and making him whimper. The pain threatened to send him under.

He fought it. He had to stay awake.

Had to stay awake.

Don't leave her alone.

Jeddy carried him away from the moonlit beach, the air around them growing darker – or was that just his vision?

Was he fading? No, he couldn't. *Stay awake.* But no matter how he tried, it was an impossible task. The moments came in flashes as James slipped in and out of consciousness.

The sting of sand being washed out of his wounds with saltwater.

A warmth on his face, the glow of a fire, broken splinters of the barrel.

His arm tended, wrapped in strips of the mock sail.

ESME.

He flinched back when he came to then, away from Jeddy, who was bent over his right arm again –

But she didn't have a knife.

No knife, no Peter.

It was safe.

Safe, he thought, as he let himself slip under.

He was being given water, but where had the water come from?

He could smell cooking meat, but hadn't the island been desolate?

After far too long a time, James awoke with enough strength in his blood that he felt he'd be able to *remain* awake. His back throbbed, but it was more a distant ache than the fire it had once been. And while his bones had an ache of their own and his stomach twisted with hunger, it only felt like being alive.

Jeddy noticed him, his feeble attempts to sit up, and propped him up against her, wordlessly handing him a piece of cold fish. They were in the mouth of a cave, facing out toward the open sea. The sun was just beginning to rise behind them, casting yellow light onto the water. Had it only been one night since they'd come ashore? Or longer?

Looking around, James guessed that it'd been a few days at the least. Enough time for Jeddy to set up a makeshift camp. He was laid on a torn piece of canvas, and that seemed to be laid over some kind of vegetation, a layer of protection between him and the sandy stone of the cave. The dying embers of a fire glowed nearby, and next to that, the barrel had been broken apart, the one remaining end turned into a bowl of sorts and filled with water.

She'd done it all alone, with him as nothing more than a burden, an invalid to be worried about while she tried to survive.

"S-sorry," James said. It hurt to talk. "S'my fault you're out here."

Jeddy only shook her head, her brown eyes sad. She brought forward the waterskin she kept at her hip and held it out to him, and he drank.

"I'm sorry," he said again when he finished, and again she said nothing, only tapping the piece of fish in his hands. He took the hint and began to eat.

"Where'd the water come from?" James asked, and Jeddy gestured to the cave behind them. So they were lucky enough to have some sort of spring.

"The plants?" he asked, and she pointed to the ceiling, bare stone. It took a moment to realize what she meant, that there had to be some sort of foliage growing on the rocks far above them. How long had it taken her to climb there? Had she been afraid of falling, of breaking a leg or hitting her head while she was alone on the cliffs?

"And ... you've been able to catch fish," James said, more in an attempt to curb his thoughts than anything else. Jeddy nodded, pointing to the far side of the cave, where a net he hadn't seen before lay on the ground, twisted from the ropes that had circled the barrel.

It didn't seem like she wanted to make conversation, and he couldn't find fault in that. She was still mourning the loss of the ship, a home taken from her because of him. "I'm sorry," he said again. "For ... for all of this."

"Ain't your fault," she replied in a quiet voice. It was the first time he'd heard her speak since the *Merry*. "Nobody's fault but Peter's."

James wanted to argue, say if only he'd drowned, if only he'd bled out on the mast, if only he'd died *weeks ago*, she wouldn't be here, wouldn't have to suffer so much.

But she was right.

It was all Peter.

"I'll kill him," he said, and it felt ridiculous to make such a statement in the state he was in, but he *meant* it. What else could he do for her? What else did he have to offer in return for all she'd done for him?

"I'll kill Peter if it's the last thing I do. I'll kill him, and you can go home."

There was something like surprise on Jeddy's face. "C-captain – " she began, but James shook his head.

"Not anymore." He took a breath. "Jeddy ... I owe you my life. Many times over. And that is not something I'll ever be able to repay, but I need to ask for one more favor. Help me get well. Help me take back my strength, and I will give you back the *Merry*." One more fight, against an enemy that had taken everything from him, for someone who deserved all he had left to give.

"And what about you?" she asked after a moment.

He sucked in air through his teeth. "That'll be it for me, I suppose."

"Sir – "

"James," he corrected her. "Even ... even if I survive Peter, there's no use for me on a ship like the *Merry*. She's an adventurer." He managed to smile. "Better served with two hands intact."

Jeddy was silent for a long moment. Did she want this? He couldn't tell if she was happy, sad, angry, or some mix of them all. He felt the same. Weak as he was, the thought of standing again, of facing Peter, of striking his tormentor down, filled him with a mixture of joy and terror. He couldn't think of anything he wanted more in the world than to take Peter out of it before he could hurt anyone else.

Before he found the supposed fountain of youth and became able to inflict his miseries *forever*.

"Alright," Jeddy said at last. "I'll help you take on Peter. But only on the condition that you *do* survive him."

James looked up at her, puzzled, and was surprised to see the shadow of a smile on her face.

"It's as you said. I saved your life many times over. Ain't about to have that be for nothin'. You survive Peter, and you stay with the *Merry*. Swear it, and I'll help you."

"Jeddy – "

"Swear it."

James clenched his jaw. What good would he be aboard? Even if removing Peter was enough to reinstate him as captain, who would follow a man that couldn't tend the ship properly? Who would obey the orders of a man they'd seen *beg*?

"James."

He met Jeddy's eyes, and her expression was intense.

"I ... I swear it," he said, swallowing. "I'll fight him to the death. And I'll win."

10

FAIRLY STRAIGHTFORWARD

Their skull-faced island was a lucky one, it seemed.

Though barren and foreboding at first glance, it had proven to hold its own treasures. It was larger than James had initially thought, with deep caves and a proper forest on the side that faced the mainland. He wasn't much help with collecting firewood or looking for food, but did his best to tend the fishing net and the fire with his one good hand. Jeddy brought in fish and fruits the likes of which James had never seen before, and once he'd regained enough strength to walk, she showed him the spring, just twenty steps past the mouth of the cave.

It took several days of good rest and food to get James back on his feet, but Jeddy was patient. The first time he stood, it was with her arm around him, and he'd leaned on her heavily as they made a small circle around the cave. It grew easier from there. Because he now had a goal, a reason. Because he owed it to Jeddy to see her home.

His strength grew a little each day, and he learned ways to move around the pain rather than through it. His ankles were scarred from his time spent in chains, and the still-healing wounds on his back kept him sleeping on his stomach, but he was adapting to the new shape of his body, spirit emboldened by sunlight and the absence of Peter's smile.

"What has Peter told you about this place?" James asked one evening. By his count, it had been two weeks since they'd been cast off the *Merry*. The smaller island provided them with all they'd needed thus far, but the land for which Peter had turned to treachery remained a mystery to him.

"Hm?" Jeddy looked up from where she'd been mending the net, tying and retwisting the bits of rope that had broken apart.

"The island," James said. "Peter's not a man of quiet excitement, and I'm sure he had plenty of stories to go around, myth or true."

Jeddy nodded at his words. "That he did. Can't say I listened to 'em all, but he had a good few." She put the net aside and set to sharpening her makeshift knife, formed from one of the metal hoops on the barrel. Her ingenuity never ceased to amaze him; she could turn something meant to mock them into the tools that may well have saved his life.

"He called it the neverland," Jeddy said. "A place where magic still runs wild, where the fae and the merfolk play wargames and the animals are clever as people."

"And do you believe any of that?"

After a moment, she nodded. "And mind you," she said, "I'd normally be as much a skeptic as I imagine you are, but this morning … " She drew up her waterskin and began to remove its stopper. "T'was almost empty, so I figured I'd wash up with what was left. And when I started pouring it out, it … well." She turned it upside down, and James watched as it flowed from the skin to the ground, soaking the sand. And it … *kept* flowing. The water kept pouring from the mouth as if it were a natural body, long after the small container should've been emptied. Once she was sure she'd made her point, Jeddy righted the skin and replaced the stopper, handing it to James.

It was still full.

"What … ?"

"I dunno. Dunno what it is or why it is, but Peter said there was magic, and after that … " She took the skin back, tucking it at her hip. "I think I believe him."

James sighed, watching the water she'd poured on the ground begin to dry up. There was magic here, he no longer had room to doubt it. But did that make every legend true? The fountain of youth, Peter's true destination, sat heavy in his mind, darkening it with the thought of Peter staying young and healthy forever, causing any harm he wished until someone managed to strike him down. It had been long enough since their arrival that he might've already found it.

No matter, James told himself. If stopping Peter from reaching the fountain was out of the question, he'd just have to stop him from leaving the island. He'd kill him if he could, but if his treacherous first mate managed to come out on top, he'd need a plan in the reserves, a way to trap him here.

The *Merry*.

The fountain was inland. Peter would have to dock her, and if James and Jeddy could reach her before his expedition returned, they could take away his only means of leaving this place. One way or another, James would make sure Peter never got a chance to spread his cruelties.

"Y'aren't strong enough yet," Jeddy said when he brought it up, shaking her head. "Even if we cobble together a raft to get there, I don't want you falling overboard."

And so they waited, eyes always on the horizon, anticipating the day when *The Scarlet Merry* journeyed out to sea again. Should that day come before James was ready, he'd have no choice but to take up a weapon and go.

Weeks passed with no sign of the ship. Or Peter, for that matter. In the moments between watching for her red sails, James spent his time walking for as long as he could, then running when simply taking the next step no longer posed a challenge. Jeddy helped him massage the scar tissue on his chest and back to prevent it from bunching his skin too tightly as it healed, and at her insistence, he practiced simple tasks one-handed.

Sharpening the knife and laying out firewood, mending the nets and gutting the fish, foraging and even swimming. It was all done carefully and painstakingly slow, but he worked at it all the same, Peter's smug grin in the forefront of his mind.

It was all for Peter. Once his enemy was gone, he could stop, he could let himself fade away, but right now he had to grow strong, adapt, if he wanted to stand a chance at bringing the other man down. That was the thought that drove him, that pushed him to run until he was on the verge of passing out, to tread water until his limbs were burning with exertion. To wake up every morning.

The thought of vengeance, and more than that, the thought of justice, of doing right by Jeddy. And beneath even those, in a part of his mind James refused to acknowledge, there was the thought of what would happen if he lost.

If he faced Peter, but wasn't strong enough to beat him. If Peter won, but didn't kill him. If the little golden crocodile came back to rest its teeth on his flesh.

Can I cut out your eye?

It wouldn't happen. He wouldn't *let* it happen. He'd die first, fighting Peter to the final breath.

***

"Y'think they might be lost?" Jeddy asked one morning, several weeks after their last sighting of the ship. "Or dead?"

"I don't know," James replied. "They may be. I'm sure we'll find out soon enough."

The two of them had begun to build a raft, gathered branches and grasses woven together an inch at a time.

"And what if they sailed around the island? Disappeared into the eastern seas?"

James shrugged. "Maybe." Not if he could help it. What would they do if *The Scarlet Merry* and her crew were nowhere to be found? There would be no way off the island, no way back to familiar waters. Jeddy's home would be lost. She knew it too. He could hear it in her voice.

"I'd wager Peter's still exploring," he said, in an effort to ease both her worries and his own. "You heard his stories. Why leave his neverland so *soon*, whether he's found the fountain or not?"

Jeddy nodded, frowning as she twisted another bundle of grasses into place. "Say it all goes well then. Say we find the ship, and no one's aboard. We can't sail her with only two, can we?"

James cursed under his breath. If it had been months ago, if he were still whole, maybe they could manage it. But as it were ...

"We don't know she's empty. Peter may have left some to keep watch," he said. "How many of the sailors aboard would be willing to abandon him?"

Jeddy sighed, running her fingers over their work. "Many were ready for an adventure into uncharted waters when he first started talkin' about the neverland," she began. "But once he took command ... once they heard what he'd done with you, seemed a lot of 'em regretted that choice."

"Didn't do much about it," James muttered, turning his attention back to his work, steadying the rushes between elbow and knee and tying with his hand. His one hand. The crew could've stopped it at any time. Staged a mutiny of their own to save him from the torment, but it had only ended at the command of their new captain.

"They were afraid," Jeddy said. "If one man tried, if no one else was brave enough to stand up with him, would he be tortured for his insubordination? No one wanted to chance it."

No one. No one, except ...

"You did," he said softly, and she went silent for a moment, her fingers stilling, gaze lingering on the mat.

"Wasn't enough," she replied.

"It was," he said. "I'm alive, am I not? I'm only here now because of you."

She seemed to grow bashful at his words, shifting in place, a smile pulling at her lips. "Suppose that's something."

The quiet grew between them for a long moment before she continued, her hands suddenly setting back to work on the rushes. "Afraid or not, I don't think any of the men are bound by loyalty to Peter."

"And what about loyalty to me?"

"Y'hear any cheers when Peter was whippin' you?" she replied. A twinge of pain went through his back, as if his body was trying to recall.

"I think we can get a few," Jeddy continued, and James nodded along, staring down at his side of the raft and trying to push away memories.

"We'll go to the *Merry* first," he said. "If anyone's aboard, we'll try and convince them, and if not, I suppose we'll go ashore. Look for Peter."

Get rid of him once and for all.

"How do we find him?" Jeddy asked. "M'not even sure we'd be able to find where he's docked the ship."

James looked up at her, unable to keep a grin from crossing his face as the realization struck him.

"I am," he said, straightening his back. He pushed the raft away and placed a finger over his heart. Over the X.

"Here's the fountain. There's said to be mountains surrounding it." His fingers traced the jagged ridges that had been cut into his chest, now nearly healed to scars, raised on his skin. "They'll drop anchor here," he said, moving his hand down to point at the angular cove that had been cut into his ribs. He traced the line upward from there, the path Peter had carved in flesh and blood.

"And if we don't find anyone at the *Merry*, the path of travel is fairly straightforward."

11

— · —

DO OR DIE

After sunset, once stars began to scatter the sky, they set off for the neverland. With only a raft, it would take hours before they reached the cove, but it would be worth it even just to see the *Merry* again. They brought their supplies along: fruit and cold cooked fish, the net, Jeddy's endless waterskin and makeshift knife, and a few sharpened sticks.

And one more thing.

"Made this for you," Jeddy had said, just before they pushed off. She'd pressed something into his hand. Metal and wood and leather. *"It's a lousy replacement, I know, and I don't think you can put much weight on it, but I'd say it's better than nothin'."*

James fiddled with the end of the device as he sat on the raft, testing the leather that secured it to what remained of his left arm, giving him something that could stand for a hand: a makeshift hook.

The remnants of the barrel hoop had been shaped and twisted, held together by wood and hardened by fire and connected to strips of leather that Jeddy must've cut from her own jacket. It was almost comforting to have its weight at the end of his arm, a feeling like a memory.

The air around them grew cooler as the hours passed, the water shining with the gentle light of the moon. Little by little, the shore of the neverland crept closer as their raft bobbed on the waves. And then all of a sudden, there she was. *The Scarlet Merry*, silent and cloaked in starlight.

James could've wept with joy. *She was still here.* Their plan could work. He looked over his shoulder and saw Jeddy, staring up at the ship with shining eyes, and he reached down to squeeze her hand. She gave him a nod, determination setting in on her face. It was time to act.

They got the raft up to the hull, close enough that he could touch the wooden planks that formed her if he wanted, and Jeddy stood, reaching up to take hold of a gunport. He watched her scale the side nimbly, agile as a cat, then waited, holding his breath until she lowered a rope for him.

Something ached inside him as he took hold of it, a voice that mourned what he'd lost. Once upon a time, he'd have no problem climbing up on his own. He could've even matched Jeddy's ascent.

And Peter took that from him.

Anger rose within him at the thought, but he pushed it back, thinking instead of the weeks behind. He'd learned to gut fish with one hand, to swim and mend with one hand. He could learn to climb too. He just needed to survive Peter.

James wrapped the rope around his hook, seizing it tightly with the other hand and giving it a tug to let Jeddy know he was situated, then he simply held on while she slowly, slowly raised him to the deck. All was quiet as he climbed over the side, no movement aside from Jeddy tying the rope in place in case they needed a quick exit. It would serve them to escape the *Merry* herself, but once aboard the raft they'd be slow in the water. It was do or die now.

Together, he and Jeddy moved about the ship, checking each cabin and finding no one.

"She's empty," he muttered. "We'll have to follow their path ashore."

"Wait," Jeddy replied, changing her direction suddenly. Heading for the brig, he realized, and followed.

James made it nearly halfway down the stairs before suddenly finding himself frozen, unable to move forward or back. The memory of the last time he'd been here – dragged up to the deck by cruel men, half-dead, wishing someone would finish the job – caught in his chest like a fish in a net.

His heart pounded, blood thrumming in his ears, making his head spin, his breath catch. His knees threatened to buckle, and he had to flatten his palm on the wall to keep from toppling over.

Stop it, he told himself. *There is no danger here. Peter isn't here.*

He felt like a fool, cowering from memories, but pushing them away felt like trying to slow the tide with a hand. They just kept washing back over him, threatening to drown him.

"James ... ?" Jeddy's voice came from the bottom of the stairs, and he gave her a jerky nod when she cast a backward glance.

"Let's get on with it," he said.

She pushed the door open, and he could hear something shift on the other side, the scrape of chain on wood. The sound sent a chill through him, and he once again fought to keep his legs.

"James?" Jeddy's voice drifted up to him again. "I'm gonna need your help with these locks."

It took a moment for her words to register, for him to realize that he'd need to take another step down the stairs, to sink deeper into his old hell. When he tried, he found his body was rigid.

Go on, move, he scolded himself. *It's nothing. You're letting yourself be spooked by shadows.*

But even when he managed to take those downward steps, he couldn't keep the sick dread away, couldn't silence his mind as it spoke against all sense; *if you go back in, who's to say how long it will be before you're let out? Will you ever come out again?*

He clutched the doorframe, leaning heavily on it. He tried to breathe deeper, to still the rising fear, but even just the smell of the place was sickening.

"S'wrong?" Jeddy asked, and James couldn't find the words to explain.

How could he say he was afraid of a room? He just shook his head. Gently, without another word, Jeddy took his hand and gave it a small squeeze.

"It's alright," she murmured. "Door's unlocked. We'll leave it that way."

Door's unlocked. James took a shaky breath, nodding with more vigor. *The door's unlocked, the chains are gone. You're standing and stronger, and Jeddy is beside you.*

Still clutching her hand, he stepped into the brig, its walls dimly lit by the glow of a lamp Jeddy'd taken from topside. The room seemed foggy and unfocused. It took another moment of silence, another moment of breathing, before James could take in what his former prison now held.

On the floor, chained ankle and wrist, sat Fiver, the cook, and Scrap, the boatswain's apprentice. Neither looked too worse for wear, and both seemed very surprised to see him.

"Captain?" Scrap said, chains rattling as he moved to stand up. "You're ... you're alive."

Captain. Maybe he could be. Maybe.

"Where's Peter?" James asked, kneeling by Fiver and getting a look at the cuffs that bound him. They could try picking the locks or just break the hinges outright, both options he hadn't had the luxury to consider during his own time down here. He wanted to break them. Smash them apart and throw them into the sea, set free two more prisoners of Peter.

"Went back to explore," the cook replied as James set to work on the locks, doing his best to keep his focus on the words, on the metal in his hand.

"Back?"

"Aye, he locked us down here not two days ago. Said he had more to see," Fiver replied.

"And why did he lock you two away?" Jeddy asked. Both men were quiet, exchanging a brief look.

"Peter found the fountain – " Fiver began carefully.

"He killed Cotts," Scrap cut him off. "He wanted to see if the water could raise the dead, so he killed her." A fierce gleam came to his eye as he continued. "I tried to fight him, Fiver too, but the others held us back and now we're here."

"I'm sorry to hear it," James said. "Cotts was a good sailor." For a moment, the only sound was the clink of metal. He meant it, that he was sorry. The feeling of betrayal lingered, the knowledge that his entire time down here, neither man had tried to help him, but he understood. Peter was a man to be feared, and carrying on as if nothing had changed was the simpler path. The safer path. He could neither praise nor fault them, but they were here now, enemies of his enemy.

"Is everyone else with Peter then?" Jeddy asked once she'd removed Scrap's restraints.

The sailor nodded. "He made it clear. Those loyal to him could drink from the fountain. Stay young forever. Those not … " He shrugged, gesturing to the room around him.

James finished working Fiver's chains and helped the cook to his feet with his good hand. His hook had been surprisingly helpful, able to keep the cuff still while he worked.

"We can finish this conversation topside," he said. "I'm sure you two would like to eat something." And James didn't want to spend another second down here. If everything went according to plan, if the *Merry* were to be his once more, he'd lock the doors of the brig for good. The tension within him ebbed away as they climbed the stairs, the constriction in his chest fading, allowing him to breathe deeply once more.

"What've you seen on land?" Jeddy asked as they went. "Were the stories true?"

"Most, from what I could tell," said Fiver. "Even caught a glimpse of the fair folk once. Peter's been speaking with 'em."

"Can't say that's good news," James replied. If the fae were anything like the folktales made them out to be, they'd make a powerful enemy. With any luck, he'd never have to deal with them.

Jeddy took the lead, opening the galley doors and rummaging around for a bit before coming back with hard biscuits and dried meat. While the men ate, James made his way inside. Toward his own cabin.

The last time he'd set foot inside it, he hadn't an inkling of what Peter was planning. It felt strange returning to it now, like stepping into a memory. James wished he could. Travel back to the night before the mutiny and warn himself, throw Peter overboard, stop the violence before it even started.

But that was only wishful thinking. He was where he was now, body carved by Peter into something broken, mind shaped into something that found fear in sounds and smells and spaces, so that he couldn't breathe easy in a room on his own ship. Nothing could be done to change what had happened. All he could do was find a way to mend, to put the pieces back where they belonged to the best of his ability. A feat he'd already begun on the skull-faced island, helped along by Jeddy. His body would never again be what it once was, but it was no longer as broken as Peter had left it. He still had room for healing, body and mind.

His cabin was largely unchanged, save for a few of Peter's things strewn over the narrow bed. James popped the lid on the trunk in the corner, sifting through his belongings until he found clean clothes. Replacing what he had on proved a bit difficult with one hand, but he managed after a few tries with help from his hook. He was struck by how good it felt to be wearing a shirt again, to replace his ragged trousers and slip on a pair of boots.

He hoped Jeddy's things were still onboard and untampered. She'd probably appreciate a change of clothes as well. In case she couldn't find her own, James pulled a linen shirt from his chest to give to her after he finished dressing. He clumsily added a belt and cutlass to his waist, then opened the door to leave.

Dawn was breaking outside, coloring the sky a pale pink. James scanned the deck until his gaze landed on Jeddy. She was oddly still, eyes wide and urgent. It wasn't until he'd begun to walk forward that he saw the man crouching behind her, the point of his knife resting on the side of her throat.

No ...

James looked about wildly, taking in Scrap and Fiver by the bow, kept motionless by the daggers at their necks. His fingers loosened, the new shirt slipping from his grasp to land in a heap on the deck.

Three sailors that he could see, all of them barely more than strangers, men they'd picked up at the last port to help tend the ship. Men that had no reason to listen to him.

Seven hells, why couldn't he have just a touch more luck? He'd been so close, why did things have to fall in Peter's favor?

Only three, but the others were unarmed. If he tried anything, it would only get their throats cut.

"Let them go," he said, his voice low and hard.

The sailors answered his demand with broad grins and snickers, and he saw Jeddy shaking her head, saw she wasn't staring at him, but past him. *Above him.*

Laughter came from somewhere far overhead.

"Give me one good reason why I should, and maybe I'll consider it."

It was Peter.

And he was flying.

12

STEEL ON STEEL

"I'll be honest, James, I thought I'd seen the last of you."

Peter had touched down on the deck and was now strutting around, the only person aboard who dared to move. His little polished knife was drawn, the crocodile engraved in its hilt seeming to taunt James with a grin.

You almost had it all. Don't you feel the fool?

"Coming back to the ship too? *Exciting*. Were you going to steal it?" He laughed. "I've been far from bored here, but if I were, leave it to you to keep things interesting."

"Are you going to kill us?" James asked. He'd had enough of Peter's theatrics. With Jeddy and the others under threat, he couldn't rush in and attack, and if he were to die without even getting the *chance*, he'd prefer to die before Peter began another soliloquy.

"Kill you? Hm." Peter tapped his chin with his free hand. "I suppose I could. But I also could not. What do you think? Should I?"

James felt his upper lip pull back into a snarl at the other man's careless tone, agitation and fear spinning as one within him. Was this a trap? Another game? If James said no, how long would he – *they* – suffer for it?

"You're hesitating an awful lot for someone who seems hell-bent on survival," Peter said. "Do you want me to kill you or not?"

"I … " James grit his teeth, clenched his muscles to keep from trembling. If he said yes, Peter would waste no time in cutting Jeddy's throat. If he said no, it could mean worse things, *terrible* things. There was only one way out of this. Only one way that gave him a chance.

"I want to play a game," James said.

Peter's eyes lit up. "Oh?" His smile grew wider, his hand tightening around the little knife. "What sort of game?"

"A contest. Between you and me. A fight," James said, straightening. A game where he wasn't tied down, where he had a weapon, where he wasn't facing impossible odds.

"A fight!" Peter seemed delighted with the idea, his feet not even touching the deck as he closed the distance between himself and James. "If you win, you'll want your ship back, I suppose. No matter. I've found I like this island quite a lot. I'm not sure I'll ever leave. And if I win – "

"If you win, you live," James said. It felt so *good* to cut him off. "Did I not mention? This fight will be to the death."

Peter seemed caught off-guard at his declaration, but a moment passed, and a different sort of smile crossed his face. Something dark, something that almost made James regret his words.

"To the *death*? Alright."

"Feet on the deck," James added quickly. "No flying." He lifted his chin. "To ... to keep it interesting."

Peter nodded, thoughtful. After a moment, he held out his hand for James to shake. *Left hand.* James thrust forward his hook, undeterred.

"I accept your challenge."

***

Peter kept the knife. There were other weapons onboard, James knew, but Peter kept the knife.

Was it overconfidence? Or was he trying to get in James's head? He felt unsettled already, with the shadowy mischief on Peter's face, but with the addition of the knife in his hand ...

He stopped himself. It was cutlass against knife, and he had the advantage. Peter was giving up both reach and power, and for what? To *taunt* him? It would be his downfall.

Jeddy and the others were now seated on the deck, sidelined while Peter's men stood sentinel to ensure they stayed that way. Blades in hand, James and Peter circled each other, watching and waiting to see who would dare to make the first move.

Cutlass against knife, James reminded himself. Victory was in reach, and then he'd knock that horrible golden beast into the sea and throw its master after it.

Peter lunged, quick enough that James was hardly able to sidestep him. So far, he was keeping his word. So far, he wasn't flying.

He darted forward again, and this time James parried with the cutlass, sending the knife gliding harmlessly past him with a satisfying *shting*.

He could do this. He wasn't in the brig, chained and helpless. He was on his feet, and he was *stronger*.

Peter was easily bored, and James was patient. If he could avoid attacks until Peter wore himself out, he'd be certain to win. Even if the other man backed out of the deal and tried to run, James could chase him. Hunt him down while he was weakened by exhaustion. End this.

He dodged another swipe from Peter. His opponent seemed to be growing frustrated, though the half-crazed grin remained planted on his face.

"What are you waiting for, James? This is your game. Won't you come play it?"

He'd have to act carefully. Ignore Peter's calls until the other man grew reckless, but engage him before he grew bored and started playing dirty.

"*James*," Peter sang. "Did you hear me?"

Another viper-quick strike, another parry from James.

And the next time Peter darted in, James followed him back out, swinging his weapon with a practiced ease. Peter managed to block each slice with his knife, the sound of metal striking metal cutting through the hush of the waves, the breaths of the men.

Even with just one move on the offense, James could feel himself tiring, the scars that covered his body pulling at him, aching with the movement. His time in the brig would not be so easily forgotten. But neither would his time on the island, and neither would his goal.

He pushed forward again, arcing the cutlass overhead, cutting into nothing as Peter tumbled out of the way. His enemy regained his footing, rushing him from the side only to be diverted with another flash of James's blade.

The blows came in a flurry then, strike after strike, steel on steel, the metallic sound ringing through the air like a sort of music.

Before the mutiny, before he'd had his strength stolen and had to rebuild it from the ground up, James had been the better fighter of the two. Now they were more closely matched. James's skill and power hadn't faded, only weakened, and stepping back into combat was like stepping into a dance he knew by heart. Still, Peter was quick, every movement fluid and agile, and James couldn't quite manage to land a blow.

He was slowing. They both were, really. Breathing heavy, taking longer pauses between each strike. James knew he had to end this soon. His endurance couldn't hold up to Peter's, not anymore.

He surged forward, swinging with a sort of frenzy, summoning all the energy he could. Overhead, left side, sweep the legs, slash at the stomach –

At long last, a stroke hit home, a shallow cut across Peter's ribcage that his opponent had been too slow to dodge completely. The sight of the blood welling up from it filled James with a renewed vigor and he stepped in, landing another hit, *another.*

Small cuts, but victories nonetheless.

Peter was wearing down.

The smile had vanished from the other man's face, his knife nearly a blur as he parried all he could with the little blade. He was all defense now, nothing able to be spared for an attack, but James refused to slow.

He half expected Peter to turn tail and flee, to take to the skies once it was apparent he could not win, but to his credit, he remained grounded. *Playing by the rules of the game.*

James poured his remaining strength into his attacks, backing his opponent into the railing of the ship, knocking the little knife from his hand, and finally, finally delivering a fatal strike.

The cutlass swept across Peter's throat, leaving a trail of red in its wake. Blood flowed freely from the wound, soaking into Peter's shirt. James took a step back as his opponent's chin dropped, letting his cutlass fall to the deck with a clatter.

It was over.

Exhaustion was already beginning to overtake him, leaving him lightheaded as he tried to catch his breath.

It was over.

"James ... " Jeddy's voice came from across the deck, and it sounded like a warning. She and the others were still seated, the sailors guarding them showing no signs of moving. *Seven hells*, he hoped he didn't have to fight them off as well –

"*James!*"

His blood ran cold as he heard a wooden creak behind him. He hardly dared to turn, but he did, and there was Peter.

Blood poured from his mouth, from the gaping wound in his throat, but he was smiling, like some horror from beyond the grave. James could only watch as he pulled a leather flask from his belt, unstopped it with his teeth, and drank.

Water mixed with blood to leak from the wound. Slowly, the gash on Peter's throat began to close, flesh and cartilage knitting together as James looked on, frozen in terror.

It was over. It was over, it was over, *why wasn't it over?*

Peter replaced the flask at his hip, and James dropped to his knees as the other man picked up the little knife. Unable to fight, unable to even flee.

Why couldn't it be over?

A sob escaped him as Peter moved to stand over his bowed form, twirling the little knife between his fingers.

"It's a funny thing," Peter said, his voice thick, muddled. He coughed, sending droplets of blood to the deck. "When one hears tell of the fountain of youth, one doesn't always *anticipate* the other gifts the water can give."

James could barely hear him over the blood rushing in his ears. It had been a fight to the death. Peter could still kill him. Peter had to kill him, *he had to.*

"After all, what good is it to be young forever when you're fragile? A reckless game can shatter a person, keep them from ever playing again or end them forever, and that's no fun." He smiled. "The neverland understands that."

"Please," James whispered, and Peter cocked his head.

"What was that?"

"Just ... just kill me. Please, you've won, so get on with it." He hoped to *God* that was enough, that Peter would see the game through, that he wouldn't have to live through more of the torments the other man dreamt up –

"No," Peter said, and the word was as good as any killing blow.

"*Please* – " James was doubled over now, unable to see past the tears blurring his vision.

"I haven't won yet. You only win a fight to the death when someone is dead."

"So kill me!" James spat out, but he knew it was no good. Peter's mind was made up.

"When the time is right," Peter said matter-of-factly, the little knife spinning round and round and round in his hand.

James lunged forward blindly, past Peter, past the knife, fumbling for the railing, throwing himself over. Better to drown. Better to die on his own terms, to hope that Peter couldn't be bothered to dive in after him –

But he never hit the water.

Arms circled his waist and he was *flying*, the ship and the water a blur below him. He jammed an elbow backward into Peter's stomach and was released, free to sink like a stone toward the sea. The impact with the water was crushing, driving the air from his lungs, but even that wasn't enough. He felt a hand around his wrist, pulling him toward the surface, back into the air, back into the sky with a disorienting speed.

As if for good measure – either to teach him a lesson or to force him into compliance – he was dropped into the water a second time, pulled out again moments later, coughing up seawater, the rapid rise and fall beginning to blacken his vision at the corners as he was carried up, up, up.

The last thing he saw before sinking into unconsciousness was *The Scarlet Merry*, far, far below.

13

X Marks the Spot

James was bound again. Arms and legs wrapped in thick vines, curled up in the middle of Peter's camp. Not secured to anything, not yet. There was no need; Peter had too many eyes on him to worry about him trying to run.

Peter had set his hearth at the center of a mossy clearing. The trees that stood around the open area were taller than any James'd ever seen, vines decorating their many branches like lace trimmings, and dawn turned the surrounding woods hazy with mist. At the heart of it all, there was a little pool. Its water was clear, moving like a lazy river, as if it were being filled by something unseen, though it never spilt over. *Peter's fountain.*

He would've called it a peaceful place, like a scene from a fairy tale, were it not for his former crew watching him with eyes that were cold or sorry – were it not for Peter, circling around him like a vulture every time he returned to the clearing.

His tormenter hadn't made a move yet, hadn't held the knife to his flesh, hadn't even *touched* him since the flight here. Peter liked him weak, he'd figured that much out by now. Give it a few days with no food, let the feeling of dread build with each passing minute. Wait until James was desperate, hungry, nearly mad with fear. *Then* he'd act.

When one of the sailors – a man known only as Green – brought him water on the first night, James tried to refuse it. The hope he'd scavenged, the thoughts of what his life could have become *after*, had faded the moment he watched Peter's broken flesh seal. The thought of survival was beyond him now; all he wanted was escape, even if the only escape was dying of thirst.

But he couldn't quite fight the men off when they forced his head back, pried his jaw open, and poured the water in. With that path taken from him, James started taunting the other sailors, calling them turncoats, *cowards*, anything that might goad one of them into an attack. It wasn't long before someone tore off his sleeve and gagged him with it.

For days, all he could do was lay miserably on the ground and watch the goings-on of the camp, the strength he'd worked so hard to recover sapping away. There only ever seemed to be a few men around at any given time, the others coming and going constantly. Peter himself was hardly seen at all.

With nothing else to do but wait, James spent much of his time thinking. He hoped against hope that Jeddy and the two others were still alive, *unharmed*. Perhaps even sailing away, back to familiar seas. Manning a ship so grand as the *Merry* would be a challenge with only three, but he was sure they could find a way. He'd made peace with his own death, but he found nothing but sorrow at the thought of theirs. Of Jeddy's.

All he had left to hope for was her safety, her happiness aboard the *Merry*. It was either that or drown in despair. After all, what could he do? Even if he were to escape now, Peter could no longer *die*. James could never rest, save for at the hour of his own demise, and he knew a swift ending was too much to ask of Peter.

As the hours passed, James found his thoughts straying from Jeddy to his captor, dreaming of ways to kill him. *Cut off his head, stab through the heart, slice open his belly and heave out the guts.* As morbid as it was, it did something to curb the fear that ate at him every waking moment.

If he were to cut Peter apart and scatter the pieces, could he still reform? James wished he could find out, but it was too late now.

He hoped Jeddy and Fiver and Scrap were safe, a small crew, but a crew nonetheless. He hoped Peter never left the island to inflict his games on anyone else.

***

In time, the hour arrived for James to die. The camp was nearly empty, with everyone off exploring or gathering food or whatever else it was they did during the day. Everyone except Peter. As he prowled closer, James knew this would not be just another taunt, another vulture's circle. This time, he would strike.

Peter had an easy time tying James down – the latter hardly had the strength to move, let alone *fight* – and the new position left him almost completely immobilized. James willed himself to breathe steadily.

This was inevitable. It would end, it was only a matter of when. It would hurt, but *it would end*. Still, he couldn't calm his racing heart, couldn't quell the rising fear.

Let it happen, he told himself. *Scream and weep if you must. It will end*.

Peter untied the gag, and the fabric was dry in James's mouth, pulling at his tongue. He couldn't hold back a whimper as Peter unsheathed the little knife, its golden teeth sharp and ready to tear away flesh.

Inevitable.

James tried to imagine breaking free, sinking the blade into its master's throat, but all he could picture was the way the flesh would bind itself back together, the way Peter would *smile*. He clenched his jaw as the other man sliced his shirt open, tracing the scars on his chest with the blade that had formed them.

"You thought it was all just a myth," he murmured. "But look where we are now. Did you ever dream it could be real?"

James didn't dignify that with an answer, but Peter didn't seem to care.

"X marks the spot," he said, knifepoint resting over James's heart. "Do you wish you could've joined me? I suppose it was never really a choice, but do you wish it were different?"

Did he? If Peter had entered the brig all those weeks ago with a proposition instead of a knife, would he have listened? To chase a fantasy and live forever beside a traitor didn't sound like him, and even the fear of what was to come wouldn't change that.

"No," he said, and winced as Peter applied just a bit of pressure to the knife, just enough to break skin.

"Even if I offered it now?" he asked.

Only for the chance to rip out your throat.

"Never," James spat. "I'd never follow someone so ... " *Cruel.* "Dull," he finished, and the word had the intended effect on Peter.

"Dull?" An incredulous expression quickly took the place of Peter's smile. "*Dull?*"

So it *was* possible to get the upper hand while bound, after all.

"You won't even finish our game," James continued. "And I hate to admit it, but I find myself getting rather bored – " Peter's hand closed around his throat, cutting off his words and his air.

"I'll finish our game when I *want* to finish our game," he hissed, leaning in close. James's head spun with the pressure, his mouth open, fruitlessly trying to draw in a breath. The terror at not being able to do so was instinctive, but with it came a sort of relief. *Would this be it?*

No. Peter released him just as his vision began to darken, and he lay there gasping.

"You want me to finish our game?" Peter was saying, his words dulled by the pounding in James's skull. "Fine." The little knife was in his hand. "But first, I have one more question." He seized his chin, forced him to look him in the eye.

James resolved not to plead for any mercies, though he knew he was only lying to himself. Only terrible things were to come when Peter was smiling like that.

"Can I cut out your heart?"

***

James didn't delude himself with the hope it would be anything but slow.

Sharp lines were drawn into his chest one-by-one, scarlet ribbons etched over each rib, the scarred map re-carved in red. He had hoped that at least the shock of the wounds would send him under, but he knew Peter was determined to make this last as long as he could.

A scream was torn from James's throat as the other man began to peel away the strips of skin, one at a time, like picking the petals off some grotesque flower. And when that was done, when the pain from the individual wounds had blurred into a continuous fire, the knifepoint dug into a rib, sending waves of agony through him as Peter began to saw through the bone.

James writhed against his bonds, his body shaking uncontrollably as he screamed and screamed and *screamed*. To hell with trying to beg, he couldn't even *think*, much less form words. He could no longer feel his limbs, couldn't see, couldn't hear – There was nothing left but the torturous white heat of the knife, steadily burrowing deeper and deeper into his chest.

But then ...

But then it stopped.

Did it?

Or was he just too far gone to tell what was happening?

He couldn't even tell if he was still screaming or not.

Maybe this was it.

Maybe it was finally over.

He hoped to *God* it was finally over.

Dying as nothing more than a sick source of amusement wasn't the end he'd wanted, not in a hundred years, but *it was an end*, and it was better than suffering under Peter any longer.

He only wished he could've dragged the son of a bitch down with him.

James was vaguely aware of a voice, of someone kneeling at his side ... *Jeddy*, her words soft and low.

Was he dead then? Were they *both* dead?

The despair that washed over him was almost enough to rival the pain, the *agony* that grew with every ragged breath. He'd thought – *hoped* it had at least been for something. That she'd be alright, back on the *Merry* where she belonged.

"James," she said, from somewhere far away.

"I'm sorry," he tried to reply, but his voice wasn't working. What good was it to be dead if everything still hurt so much?

Something bitterly cold splashed across his exposed ribcage, and he was almost certain he screamed again at the contact.

"James," Jeddy said again, and her voice was clearer this time. "James, *please* ... "

"We need to go." Another voice, somewhere further back, low and urgent. "He won't stay dead forever."

Stay dead?

Jeddy's face was coming more into focus, and behind her, near the edge of the clearing, stood Scrap and Fiver. And behind them ...

"What ... ?" he croaked out, and found he could breathe again, that the pain was steadily ebbing away. He knew what he would see before he looked down. The fibers of bone reforming, the ruined flesh repairing itself, everything settling back into place on his bloodied chest.

Jeddy cut him free, then tucked an arm under his back, easing him up. Even the dizziness and hunger pangs were fading. He stood with Jeddy's help, looking toward the others.

Behind them, Peter lay on the ground by the tree line, body spasming, hands fruitlessly clawing at the wooden spear that went right through his throat and into the earth, pinning him there.

"Can you walk?"

He tore his gaze away from his downed enemy. "I ... I think ... " His fingers grazed his stomach, the scars there still present, but fully healed. "What did you do?"

Jeddy's eyes went to the ground. "I – I took some water from the fountain. I tried askin', but you were too bad off to answer. I didn't know what else to do, I – " She looked up at him. "I'm sorry – "

"No. No, I'm not angry," James said quickly. "I just ... " He swallowed. "You came after me. I didn't think ... "

"You're the captain," she said, like it was the most obvious thing in the world. "Can't sail off without the captain."

"Jeddy ... " He wasn't sure which of them it was that initiated the embrace, but suddenly their arms were around each other, holding on like it was the only thing anchoring them to the earth.

"Y'promised you'd come back aboard and I'll hold you to it," she said, voice thick with emotion and muffled by his shoulder.

"That I did," he replied, unable to keep the waver out of his own voice. "But I couldn't have kept that promise without the best first mate I could ask for."

It felt as if a great deal of strength had been returned to him as they pulled back from each other and made for the tree line.

He couldn't tell if it was an effect of the healing water or if it was something more.

"We'd best hurry," Fiver said, taking the lead. "Peter's boys could be back at any minute."

"Onwards then," James replied, his hand clasped in Jeddy's as they began to run. "The *Merry*'s waiting for us."

— · —

EPILOGUE: THE ENDLESS GAME

"Am I ... like him now?"

They'd made it to *The Scarlet Merry* with little trouble, but hadn't yet set sail. Safely aboard, James's focus was currently on his makeshift hook. The water had healed him, closed his wounds like they'd never happened, but left him with the scars he'd had before. Peter's map. The whip marks. The missing left hand. As if the island didn't want him to forget.

Scars or no scars, he wouldn't.

"Dunno." Jeddy stood next to him, leaning on the ship's railing. "The legends say you must drink from the fountain, but it mended you all the same." She shrugged. "Might've touched me as well, seeing as I used this to fetch it." She tapped the flask at her hip. "Never runs out, so I dunno what water's what."

"What if it did?" He let his gaze drift to the waves below. "Do you want to live forever?" If the water had done more than just heal him, if it had changed him, changed *them*, was he happy with that? The concept of forever was a difficult one,

108

a sprawling infinity that he couldn't grasp, but he imagined it would be easier if it were to be taken day by day.

"Forever at sea, forever aboard the *Merry* … " Jeddy shrugged again. "I can imagine worse fates."

They didn't leave the cove that day or the next. James knew they'd be willing to leave at any moment if he just gave the order, but something held him back.

Unfinished business.

As much as he wished the spear to the throat was enough to keep Peter down, he knew it wasn't. It would take more than that to bury his enemy, and if it was true, if he was now undying as well, he had all the time in the world to find out what 'more than that' was.

Fiver, being the cook, was the first to discover that their food stores were as endless as Jeddy's waterskin. Nothing dwindled, nothing ran out. From the crate of hardtack, to the salt pork, to the little box of cane sugar.

It seemed Peter's neverland had no short supply of gifts to give.

Days passed without any trouble, the only sign of his old crew being a few men seen flying far overhead. Scouts, no doubt. James knew it was unlikely Peter would leave them alone. It was only a matter of time before the other man decided to stage another attack, and he knew he had a choice to make.

Sail or stay?

Peter didn't want to leave the island. If they set off, even with a crew as small as theirs, there was a chance they could make it far enough that he wouldn't follow.

But what would Peter do then? What would happen in a dozen years or more, when he at last grew bored of it all? True, the neverland was a great distance from any civilization James knew of, but Peter couldn't *die*, and he was certain if the other man set his mind to it, he'd make it somewhere. Unkillable, unconstrained. God help anyone who he decided to toy with.

James couldn't let that happen. Not when it was possible he'd been granted an opportunity to fight fire with fire. If he were immortal, who better than him to find a way to stop Peter? After all, they still had a game to finish.

But he wasn't the only one aboard the *Merry*. The others had the right to choose their paths forward.

***

"I find it's become my duty to put an end to Peter," James said one night as they had their dinner. "I can't in good conscience leave this island until I know for certain he's dead."

"And what if 'dead' is impossible?" Scrap said around a mouthful of food.

"There must be a way," James replied. "And if there is, I'll find it." He ran his fingers over his hook. "I won't try and order any of you to stay by me. If you wish, take the *Merry* and sail far away from here. I won't try and stop you, nor will I think less of you for it."

He waited, the room filled with an easy silence.

"I'll stay." Jeddy was the first to speak. There was a slight smile on her face, a warmth in her eyes. "What's a captain without a first mate?"

"And what's *either* of those without a cook?" Fiver added. "Can't very well let y'be cooking for yourselves."

"Suppose you'll need someone to tend the sails," Scrap cut in, then added in a softer voice, "Cotts taught me well. Hope I can do half as good a job."

A warmth grew within James, the seed of hope Jeddy had given him what seemed so long ago blooming. No matter the things they'd said before, it was only now that he truly felt like he was captain again, at last able to make his own choice and not have it be driven by survival or pure necessity. And beyond what he'd hoped for, he had people willing to stand by him in a task that may yet prove impossible.

"I couldn't ask for a better crew," he said, and meant it with all his heart.

The next day, they finally set sail. Not to flee or to seek safer harbors, but instead to circle the island in a sort of patrol. Even with land in sight, it felt freeing to be out on the water again, aboard his own ship. James found it easy to steer the *Merry* with the help of his hook, but even in fair weather, he knew looking after the ship was a struggle for only three.

So he sat down with Fiver and Scrap, coming up with a list of those who weren't fully loyal to Peter, who may yet be swayed to come back aboard *The Scarlet Merry*. James made another silent promise, right beside his vow to see his enemy to the grave: he'd find his former crew, however long it took, and make sure each sailor at least had a choice.

By day they sailed, singing the old shanties that somehow sounded just as full as they had when sung by dozens instead of four. By night they let the ship drift, sleeping or watching the stars. Jeddy was right. There were worse fates than living forever at sea.

And when Peter at last made his appearance, piercing the air overhead like a bird of prey, James was not afraid.

***

Years passed like days. Time was easily lost in the eternal summer of the neverland. James could sail the island's waters blind. By now he knew them like the back of his hand. Like the scars on his torso. The *Merry* thrived in these waters, never faltering, never wearing even when she should. In time, some of the sailors in Peter's band left him, returning to her. *Returning home*.

Peter came too. Came and went, fought James, fought Jeddy, fought any sailor who crossed his path. Sometimes Peter died. Sometimes James died.

But they always came back for the next battle. Even Peter's little knife couldn't put a stop to that.

It was a curse, a blessing. It was a game that never ended.

"What happens if you beat him?" Jeddy asked one evening. They'd tried to bargain with the merfolk earlier that day, seeking more knowledge of the fountain and finding very little.

"If I beat him?"

"For good," she added. The moon was full, casting a soft glow on her face and the tight coils of her hair, lighting up her eyes. He truly could not say how long it had been since they'd first come here, since those first pain-filled days at the skull-faced island. Be it one year or ten, Jeddy didn't seem to have aged a day. He supposed he'd make the same observation about himself, should he take his time in front of a mirror.

"If I should ... I suppose we could leave," James mused. "Pick a horizon and sail away. Leave the island's games behind forever." Even as he said it, he knew it would never be. The neverland was a part of them now, and they of it. Removing themselves would be no different from ...

From separating a man from his hand, James thought, the notion somehow as amusing as it was bitter. Not impossible to do, nor impossible to live with. Only strange, for a while.

"M'not sure I'd want to leave. Or even if I could," Jeddy said, voicing his thoughts.

"Whether we want to or not, the choice is a distant one. Peter is not an obstacle that will be easily buried."

"And if you can never find a way?"

"Suppose we'll be here forever then." *Forever playing Peter's game.*

Jeddy laid a hand over his. "It's not so bad a forever," she said, and he smiled.

"No. It's not."

Forever aboard his ship, his home. Forever with a good crew, with a first mate he trusted with all of his being. Forever hunting Peter, playing this endless game, and maybe, one day, he'd *win*.

It was his choice.

It was his forever.

And it was enough.

ACKNOWLEDGEMENTS

I owe a lot to the whump community for resparking my passion for writing. Without it, I don't think I'd be where I am today, and I am thankful for their support, inspiration, and friendship. I would also like to thank Nate for encouraging me to finish a project, and the Whumpy Printing Press for all the hard work they've put in to bring this collection to life!

ABOUT THE AUTHOR

Callie has loved writing since elementary school, and devotes most of her freetime to crafting some kind of world, be it with words or with art. When not creating, she enjoys hiking, rock climbing, and playing ukulele.

— · —

BEFORE YOU GO

This is the fourth book in 12 Months of Whump, a series of whumpy novellas published by WPP throughout 2025. Each novella can be read as a standalone.

To stay up to date with the 12 Months of Whump series and other whumperfly-inducing projects, visit us at https://thewhumpyprintingpress.tumblr.com/

www.ingramcontent.com/pod-product-compliance
Lightning Source LLC
Chambersburg PA
CBHW052007170626
46808CB00007B/2812